"Kurt Fawver's stories are nasty little shockers that dare to dream big. And he isn't afraid to follow those big and totally mad ideas through to their horrific conclusions. Yeah, Kurt is a little messed up, and *Forever, in Pieces* is a promising debut."

—Paul Tremblay, author of *In the Mean Time*
and *Swallowing a Donkey's Eye*

"From the most far-flung reaches of space, time and imagination, Fawver presents a parade of original and startling visions."

—David Dunwoody, author of
Unbound & Other Tales

"A poignant and genuinely unnerving debut collection. Exquisite in every possible way. Kurt Fawver is a virtuoso of short-form literature, and *Forever, in Pieces* is his magnum opus."

—Adam Millard, author of *Dead Line*

"*Forever, in Pieces* is aptly titled, for this book offers readers unnerving glimpses into our eternal fears, both staggeringly cosmic and painfully intimate. Kurt Fawver's tales are gruesome and poignant. An impressive debut."

— Richard Gavin, author of *At Fear's Altar*

"With *Forever, in Pieces,* Kurt Fawver creates a collection perfectly balanced between beautiful and vicious, clever and dark. Like love stories for the dead, it calls to your soul to just keep turning pages."

— Jonathan Moon, author of *Heinous* and *Hollow Mountain Dead*

"Fawver's *Forever, in Pieces* is a searing and unapologetic exploration of futility. His very purpose in the tragically beautiful arrangement of his words is to prove that 'On every level, we are not meant to over-come; we are meant to fall apart'—and his thoughtful, captivating stories illustrate this truth in an impeccably somber literary performance."

— Shawna L. Bernard, editor of *Cellar Door* and *Ugly Babies*

Kurt Fawver

FOREVER, IN PIECES

◆

Previous Appearances:

"Brief Repose Moments Before a Gruesome and Certain Death"
Daily Frights 2012. Pill Hill Press. December 2011

"Lessons"
Daily Frights 2012. Pill Hill Press. December 2011

"Should Old Acquaintance Be Forgot"
Morpheus Tales #12. April 2011

"For the Unhaunted"
National Public Radio online—NPR.org. October 2010

"Bolt"
Zombie Nation: St. Pete. Zombie Nation Publishing. October 2010

"Birth Day"
Encounters #2. April 2010

Parts of "The Waves from Afar" originally appeared as
"Watching the Watchers"
Zombie St. Pete. Silver Tongue Media. February, 2010.

To Erin, who isn't afraid to shine a light on my malformed soul.

To my parents, who've lived long enough to see me become everything they dreamed of and everything they had nightmares about.

And to Gatsby, just because.

Introduction

I wrote my first short story when I was ten. It centered on a nameless peasant who was forced to climb a never-ending mountain in pursuit of some sort of monstrous, ultimate evil—an amorphous creature that had killed countless thousands of innocents and would kill countless thousands more if not stopped. The twist in my tale—which, at ten, I thought was pretty clever—was that the peasant couldn't destroy the beast; it was impervious to all human intervention, all forms of conventional attack. My everyman hero had to engage the creature in battle for all eternity so that the rest of humanity might be spared its wrath. This lone peasant, a virtual nobody, had to fight forever, without the hope of ever winning, without the slightest recognition or reward, so that the rest of the world might live and prosper.

Thematically, not much has changed in my writing in the twenty odd years since I scribbled that tale. Most of my stories still revolve around confrontation between utterly average people and the absolutely insurmountable. I suppose you could say it's the bedrock of my writing: banality and ineffectuality in conflict with chaos and deepest darkness. We are a species eternally trying to rise above our fragility and our fallibility, to master an indifferent or outright hostile universe, and, most often, we fail in such attempts. On every level, we are not meant to overcome; we are meant to fall apart. And yet we struggle against the inevitable collapse of all things, and it is this struggle—an ever-flowing torrent of blood and sweat and tears of both joy and sorrow—that defines human existence as it sweeps us further into an ocean of limitless possibility that we quaintly term "the future." My stories try to bottle that torrent, to provide a moment of foundational, cosmic conflict and an aesthetic feeling of simultaneous hopelessness and hopefulness for all our tomorrows, however terrifying or wondrous they may be.

Along those same lines, most of the stories in this collection circle around the idea of "forever" or "eternity." It can be a creepy idea, a thing that goes on without end. For, without an end, without a frame to encapsulate it and give it context, what meaning does a thing have? Does it ever change, or is it dead, a static monolith? And, worst of all, what price might we pay for a thing having no end? In the stories that follow, I've tried to interrogate ideas closely aligned with eternity—birth and children, religion and faith, love and longing, etc.—in an effort to more fully elaborate on what being "forever" might entail.

Many of the stories that reside on the pages beyond might also be labeled horror. But don't let that moniker fool you; horror need not entail simplistic, puerile tales of titillation (indeed, much horror is neither simplistic nor puerile). While there's plenty of splatter and shadow in my stories, my explicit intent is neither to shock nor cause bouts of nausea. No, for the most part, the purpose of my fiction is to unsettle. I want my readers to come away from my stories with a chink in their preconceptions and a tremor in their beliefs. If you're entertained by my work on a visceral level, I'm thrilled. But if my stories also force you to exercise your intellect—even just a little bit—then I've truly succeeded as a writer.

All this said, I want to sincerely thank you for reading my stories. For, without a reader, a writer is nothing more than a faucet let run in an abandoned house, endlessly pouring his or her soul down a rusted drainpipe. But you, gracious reader, by your very interest in digesting these words, you make it less likely that my writing will end up as cultural sewage. So, again, thank you for picking up this book.

Without further ado, then, let me step aside, fade into the margins, and welcome you to my debut collection of short fiction, *Forever, in Pieces.* I hope you like it.

Kurt Fawver

Tampa, Florida | July 2013

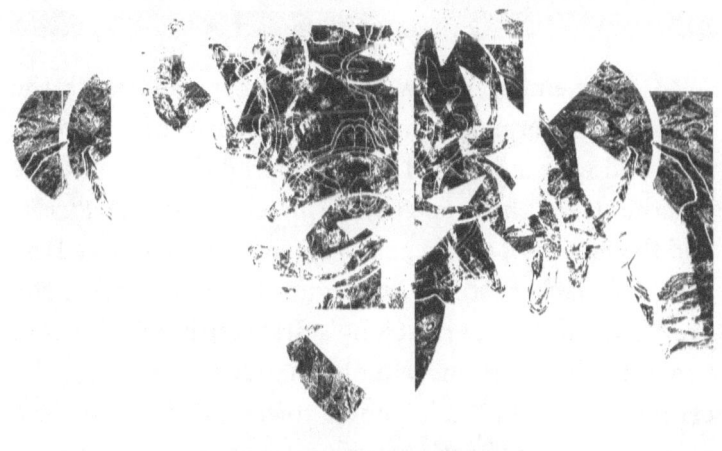

Prologue to
a Phantasmagorical Tragedy

Fifteen thousand years ago a man in a cave sat down with pen and paper, though neither had officially been invented yet, and began to write his autobiography, though written words had no meaning since they had not yet been scribbled out by the hand of humankind.

The man was lonely, and had been so for as long as he could remember, which, it happened, was a span of fifteen thousand years.

A strange thing about the man's memory, though: it marked time in reverse. He recalled not the past, but the future. Yesterday was a blurry, indistinct thing to him, but tomorrow—tomorrow was crisp and certain.

The man saw vast, as-yet unfolded sheets of time neatly pressed and stretched out before him. Fifteen thousand years of miracles and terrors fought for space behind his eyes.

He remembered how to drive a car and search the internet for floral delivery. He remembered how to load a rifle and wire a bomb. He remembered the fall of Rome and the rise of Charlemagne, the majesty of Holst's *Planets* and the horror of Hitchcock's *Psycho*. He remembered the swell of black pustules in plague-stricken Europe, the grainy video of Neil Armstrong's first step onto the moon, the gray clouds of uncertainty that swept out from the crumbling World Trade Center towers, and the smiling seas that greeted boatloads of veterans as they returned from the hellscapes of World War II. But, perhaps most importantly, he remembered everyone he ever loved dying.

The man's unborn wives and husbands, his children and friends—he remembered their cold bodies lying flat and static in holes and boxes, gone before they had ever arrived.

And this is why he wrote: not to entertain with his remarkable adventure or to guide humanity's development, but to forget that every happiness, every shred of warmth and communion, would eventually unravel and dissolve.

Every day, the man filled another page with memories that hadn't yet come to pass and every day he tried to hide his heart away inside the words. Within the words, the flow of time arrested; within the words, past and future exploded into an ever-present now. There, on paper, smiles never faded, kisses never grew stale, and grave-yards remained forever meadows.

Over months, over years, the man wrote, and his memories swam up to meet him. He starved through famine he'd starved through before and survived a bear attack he'd survived long ago. He scavenged and clawed his way through the wilderness in all the ways he already knew he would and, slowly, he penned the story he'd already written.

Then, one day, he finished. He placed the final sheet under all the rest and waited, but the future past came rushing back into his soul, and it had only one sad chapter.

So the man did what he always would. He picked up the book and began to read, because, he had no doubt, reading the present was far more comforting than remembering the future.

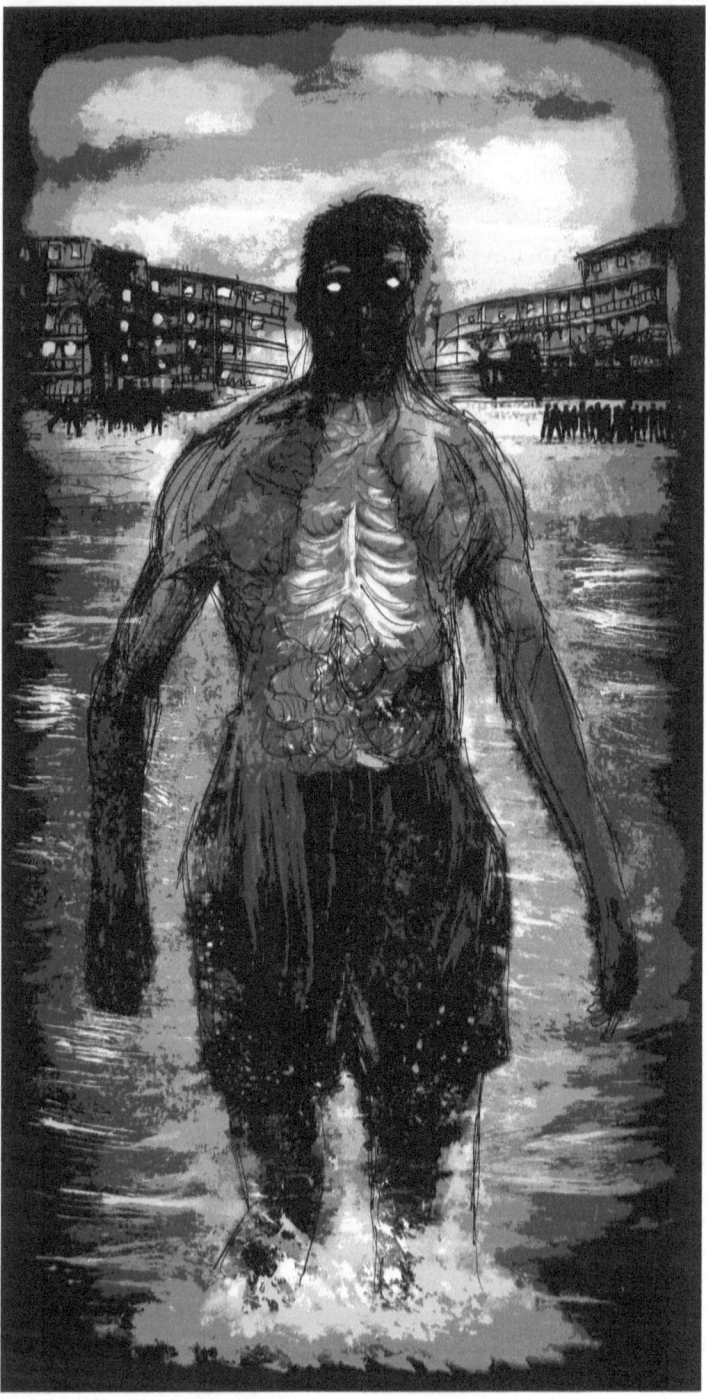

The Waves from Afar

There they stand, waist deep in the surf, staring at the horizon, letting the waves drag their failing flesh into the gentle roll of the gulf. My wife. My sons. They're only three among the thousands. They can't hear me. And if they do, they don't respond. Whatever they see now, whatever holds them in rapture here, at the epicenter of the phenomenon, is more important than all the "I love yous" I can scream.

I come here every day and watch them watching the flashes and the colors. I should drive back home. But I can't. It's too hard to say goodbye. I know they're gone and that this is nothing more than a gloriously extended funeral. They're unblinking, unthinking acolytes of the Tide now. I know that. But, still, there they are, eyes wide, wobbling in the ebb and flow as if they were actually alive and straining to maintain balance. I wish they would fall over. I want them to let go. But they won't fall. They'll stand in the same spot and stare until their legs snap and they're swept out, away from me and closer to that beautiful, frightening panorama.

What's out there? What do they see that I can't? What chain binds them to this liminal space between life and death, land and sea, being and memory? If only I knew, if only I could slide sideways just a fraction of an inch, just far enough to catch a glimpse of the view from their detached retinas, then maybe I could cut them free. Maybe somewhere beyond the waves is hope. Maybe that's what holds them here in eternal fascination.

There's no way to tell from where I sit, hunched under an umbrella on the beachhead, kicking sand into the wind. I'm not alone here. Far from it. Husbands and wives, mothers and fathers, sons, daughters, friends and lovers of every variety: they all perch high on the pure, untainted sand and wait. Some listen to music. Some watch portable televisions and DVD players. Some have picnics. Some dance. Some shriek and weep. Some curse God and some laugh. It's an odd sort of atmosphere, this mixture of revelry and apocalypse.

Occasionally, grief consumes one of my fellow mourners and he or she runs moaning into the water—a suicidal decision. Contact only needs to last ninety seconds, and there is no known cure. Two or three days following contact, the loss and insane sorrow that once overwhelmed the runner fades, along with the rest of the world. Nothing remains but a stopped heart and unabashed awe. Eventually—sometimes minutes later, sometimes days afterward—the body rises, turns toward the gulf, and shambles back to join the congregation of the eternally fascinated.

I haven't seen any newcomers today, though. Surprising. I wish I had. It forces me to think about someone else. Another situation. Another set of ruined lives. Not Cara's. Not Nick or Sammy's. Not my own.

Sitting here for over a week has been hell. I've been replaying everything in my mind on a continuous loop. The memories refuse placation. Sleep doesn't help; booze is useless; I even smoked a joint a couple nights ago, but all it did was make me paranoid that those husks in the water might actually still retain a spark of their former selves. No matter what I do, the bittersweet images won't stop kneading my thoughts. They won't be satisfied until I'm scrambling toward my family, pushing away the beach guards, and soaking in death like so many others who could no longer carry the burden of being left alone on dry land.

See, all my time spent darkly meditating has made me realize how I could've prevented this, how I could have saved my family from the Tide.

I just had to plead my case for a vacation to London. That's where I wanted to go. But I remained silent and was carried away by the familial flow.

For a month before we finalized our travel plans, Cara and the boys were in thrall to the news about the gulf—how beachgoers in Clearwater had begun noticing brightly-hued swirls of color in the water, how the CDC and EPA had closed and quarantined the shore from Panama City to Naples, how all the sealife had mysteriously vanished from the coast. It was ominous. It was mundane. It was like the first fifteen minutes of a surprisingly inspired horror movie. People stayed far away, in fear of toxins and pollution, disease and dessication.

Soon, however, the lightshows began and droves of vacationers poured back in.

The lightshows are, simply put, glowing water. The waves on the western coast of Florida, from Panama City to Naples, glow at night. That was the thing that brought vanloads of sightseers, tens of thousands of giggling children and their parents, and innumerable journalists and scientists to the area. Incredibly, undeniably, the tides burst with billions of tiny flashes—an undulating field of Christmas lights.

The effect was gradual—only a vaguely noticeable shimmer at first—but, over the course of the few weeks that the beaches were closed, the glittering points grew in number and intensity, until even the sky above the gulf was a shifting rainbow of cold chromaticity.

I have to tell you, I've never really cared for the beach. I hate the water, and irradiating my body in the noonday sun is not my idea of fun. But even I couldn't deny that the lure of luminescent water—*unexplainable* luminescent water at that—was too tempting. The boys' excitement and Cara's mischievous grin were infectious. They wanted to witness a spectacle. Secretly, so did I. The sight of the glimmering, prismatic waves was supposed to be eerie; it was supposed to be breathtaking; it was supposed to be safe.

Following two uncharacteristically short weeks of study and analyzation, the EPA and the CDC reopened the Floridian gulf shores. They declared that, although there was no concrete answer as to why the phenomenon was occurring, there were also no harmful substances in the water; everyone, from the doe-eyed toddler to the arthritic grandmother, was cleared to splash about in the rich spectrum which permeated the sea from surface to floor. People scurried to secure hotel rooms and plane tickets, all in an effort to be among the first to take the plunge into preternatural waters.

We were some of those people. Clearwater Beach, where the colors were reportedly brightest and most vibrant, was our vacation destination. Only ten short days ago—exactly one week after the beaches were reopened— we packed up the car and set off toward the southern sun.

I drove throughout the day and into the lonely witching hours of the night. Cara read. Cara slept. The boys hit each other and played Nintendo DS. When we finally arrived, it seemed that Clearwater, with its cool white beaches, was the new axis of miracles. Because I watched too much Travel Channel programming, I knew that it had always been a mecca for tourists seeking a relaxing ocean getaway, but the colored, illumined waves were the stuff of dreams and wonder; they appealed to a much broader swath of the public than mere beach-combers. As a result, psychics and UFO buffs littered the sidewalks, hawking services, wares, and fringe theories. New Age adherents wandered the streets searching for vibrations and vortexes. Curbside prophets bellowed damnation from atop benches and homemade pulpits. Amateur and professional photographers struggling to frame the kinetic socioscape meandered through the masses with lenses held aloft. And everywhere, truly everywhere, were jostling families.

I honked the horn a thousand times, gritted my teeth, and sped to our hotel as quickly as possible. After checking in, throwing our suitcases in the rooms, and grabbing some chilled drinks, we ventured out to the beach. It was only a few blocks from where we were staying, so we walked.

As we crested the tiny dunes that separated the ocean from our sight, Nick let out a startled "Whoa!" Although not religious by any sense of the word, Cara murmured "My god." Sam simply continued playing with the toy in his hand, oblivious to non-material wonder. For my own part, I froze, mouth agape, and felt a soothing blankness descend over my being.

What lay before us was unreal. It was strangely alien and intensely personal. The water had been transformed. It was as if waves of shimmering gemstones pounded the shoreline, shifting color as they rolled in. Red then blue, yellow then green. Purple. Orange. Back to red. A rippling kaleidoscope. Hypnotizing and exhilarating at once. The entire visual spectrum had been rendered into a field of fluidity; this phenomenon, whatever its cause or its purpose, was certainly more than a mere tincture in the tides. It was beauty. It was art. If I hadn't known it was the ocean—the real, phenomenal ocean—I would have sworn that the waves, which seemed to stretch out beyond the bounds of eternity, were a masterful expressionist canvas somehow charged with motion.

Cara, Nick, and Sam couldn't wait to wade in and stake out a spot next to the hundreds of men, women, and children already flailing about in the water. They practically sprinted to join the dripping throngs. I, however, was exhausted from the nonstop drive, so I found an open space among the patchwork quilt of beach blankets and sunbathers, set up a lounge chair and an umbrella, and tried to relax.

Laughter rode the breeze. The heavy sweetness of tanning lotion hung over passing bodies. My chair hugged me snugly. All was peace. All was perfection.

Except for the lack of birds.

I didn't notice at first, but there were no gulls on the shore, nor any gliding through the air over the coast. No pelicans bobbed atop the surface of the gulf, either. I knew from news reports that this was to be expected. Birds, fish, crustaceans, manatees and dolphins: the whole aquatic community had disappeared when the tides turned vibrant. But to see its effect, to experience it firsthand and realize the traumatic breadth of the chasm that had split normalcy to allow magic and wonder free passage, was wholly different than reading a website in the transparent mundaneness of my living room.

Despite the unsettling lack of fauna, I managed to drift off to sleep for maybe half an hour or forty-five minutes. No one bothered me. I was floating in a joyously extended moment somewhere between Florida and oblivion.

Then the screaming began.

At first, it was only an annoyance, an unswattable gnat buzzing in my outer ear. I awoke, grumbled, and re-adjusted my position; surely, I assumed, the ambient noise would soon return to pleasing uniformity. Any screaming must have been the result of a misbehaving child or a domestic dispute. It would subside. There was no doubt that it would subside.

But it didn't.

The screaming continued, and it grew louder, more primal, more frantic. I opened my eyes and squinted against the harsh noonday rays. Cara was sitting on a blanket beside me, staring at something in the distance; the boys had apparently been digging tunnels in the sand but had stopped to watch the same thing that held Cara's attention. I followed their gaze along the shoreline to a spot maybe fifty or sixty yards away. There, knee-deep in the sparkling rainbow water, a middle-aged woman wearing a retina-searing floral print sundress grappled with a generously tanned man wrapped in what appeared to be a pink bathrobe. The woman was alternately shrieking and sobbing incoherent words and phrases while tugging on the man's arm in what seemed to be an attempt to pull him back to the beach. He was unresponsive, though, and continued to stand frozen in place, facing the vibrantly stricken gulf. Not once did his focus shift to the woman.

The scene confirmed my suspicions of domestic disturbance.

"Trouble in paradise," I muttered to Cara.

She shook her head.

"I'm not so sure. They came from back toward the city and sprinted across the beach to the water. She was chasing him. I mean, I don't get it. Why is he wearing a bathrobe? And, look, it's only pink in the middle and the bottom. The top is white. I think he's bleeding or was around someone who was bleeding."

Cara was always more inquisitive than me. She wanted to know, to understand, to experience. I just wanted to be.

I sat up and studied the man in more detail. She was right. His robe was only pink up to the shoulders. Odd, but still, what did it matter? It was a wife and husband, fighting while on vacation. Nothing new or interesting in any way. I heard sirens in the distance but assumed no connection. Given the vast number of people that meandered on and around the beach, there was bound to be rowdy, drunken debauchery, petty crime, and minor accidents. Again, I was unconcerned.

I was about to lie back and relax when the screaming woman yanked hard on the man's arm and tore away his robe, revealing the hidden reality of his torso. It was a glistening mass of exposed muscle, fat, and bone. From the top of the man's chest to the middle of his abdomen ran a gaping wound, ragged around the edges, as if a predatory animal had gnawed at his body. I thought I saw part of a bruised purple organ—his liver or stomach, possibly—partially hanging out in the salty air.

Cara gasped and ordered the boys to "come here."

The sirens grew louder.

The tanned man seemed ignorant of his horrific injury. He did nothing other than stare unflinchingly at the horizon. I couldn't believe he was on his feet and conscious; how a person could survive an injury of such magnitude was beyond my meager comprehension.

A lifeguard and two paramedics came running from the direction of the wailing emergency vehicles. They approached the couple and immediately set to work. The lifeguard quieted the woman while the paramedics attempted to usher the man back toward dry land. He didn't budge.

A sizable crowd had begun to form around the scene and it was increasingly difficult to see what was happening as more and more gawkers came to stare. A wall of bodies teetered between my family and the couple, so what happened next I only caught in glimpses and sound bytes.

The paramedics had, apparently, tried to pick up the injured man and carry him away from the water. But they never reached dry sand. Instead, a series of frantic splashes wet the air and were immediately followed by a gristly ripping noise and a single male scream. An echoed chorus of screams burst from the dense crowd. The gawkers began scattering. I stood, but could only see the tanned man walking back into the waves, one of his hands shining red. There was more screaming.

As a pair of police officers forged their way past us, through the dispersing crowd, one of the paramedics dragged the other one, unconscious, onto the beach. Half his face was missing. His nose was a black, bubbling hole. One eye dangled from its socket. His skull was exposed entirely. I could even see his tongue working inside his mouth. By then, I couldn't think; I could only react.

I reached down, grabbed Cara's hand, squeezed, and yelled "Get Sam. We're going back to the hotel. Now."

Despite their weight, we each picked up a child and jogged away from the violence. We didn't stop until, panting and near cardiopulmonary collapse, we reached the motel.

That night, tired, angry, and confused, we sat our room and watched the news. The incident we had witnessed had played out in various forms up and down the gulf coast. Along Clearwater's beaches alone, thirty-six instances of similar "severe physical trauma" followed by "psychotic fixation on the water" had occurred. Experts assured the viewing audience that the coloration phenomenon had no bearing on these incidents.

Under the order of the CDC, all the beaches along the gulf coast of Florida were, once again, closed until further notice.

I remember standing on the tiny balcony of our motel that evening, long after Nick and Sam and Cara had fallen asleep. I looked to the west, to the sky, and I saw the full scope of the miracle. I saw the breathtaking beauty; I saw the alienness; I saw what was to become the symbol of pure horror. And I was mesmerized by it. The tides lit the firmament and blotted out the stars. In the glowing bursts of primary color, I wondered if God existed. I wondered if I existed.

I knew there were no answers.

A day passed and news crews swarmed Clearwater, interviewing anyone with an opinion. Dire rumors began circulating across the internet. People came forward with startling information. Self-identified family members and friends of the violent beachgoers claimed that their unfortunate loved ones had contracted a disease that dissolved organic tissue. The phrases "flesh-eating bacteria," "radioactive waste," and "acidic pollution" were all batted about. The disease, these people said, began as a tiny spot of irritation—like a bug bite—but quickly developed into a full-blown invasion of the body, consuming flesh and muscle as it went. Nerve fibers, said the families and friends, were left untouched. Medical personnel who had treated the apparently infected individuals remained silent.

Darker yet were the stirrings in the depths of the digital sea that suggested that the infected had, in fact, succumbed to the illness before bolting for the gulf. Reanimated dead, some said. Zombies.

Ridiculous.

Impossible.

Impossible as unexplainable glowing waves.

Cara and the boys and I drove south to St. Petersburg and took in a Rays game that second day. It wasn't on our itinerary, but both Cara and I needed to put some distance between ourselves and the gulf. Nick and Sam didn't care one way or the other. To them, new was new, interesting was interesting; they didn't carry the weight of multiplicitous signification yet.

While we were at the game, several hundred more people had wandered into the water off Clearwater beach in what was being called "a dazed, near-catatonic state." The CDC wrangled them all and placed them in quarantine at an undisclosed location.

We ate at a pizza buffet for dinner. I kissed Cara and hugged the boys. We talked about pirates and sea monsters. We laughed. This was our vacation.

That night, Nick woke from a fitful sleep and complained that he felt tingly. Cara found a bright yellow spot on his shoulder unlike any rash or pimple or insect bite I'd ever seen. Near dawn, I heard Cara vomiting in the bathroom. Sammy slept for sixteen hours.

And still hundreds more limped and shuffled their way into the waves.

The National Guard was called in to barricade the beach; they stretched out lines of razor wire and posted armed sentries every five hundred feet. Even with these precautions, droves of the potentially comatose or possibly dead managed to slip through undetected. Footage from news helicopters revealed that the number of "watchers," as they had been labeled by the media, was growing exponentially. On the beaches of some of the more populous coastal cities and towns, they stood elbow to elbow.

The third afternoon of our vacation, we played miniature golf and licked ice cream cones. Nick kept scratching his back. Cara rushed to the restroom several times. Sam barely moved. After dark, we saw a new Pixar movie and gazed at the illuminated sky. We all spoke in hushed timbres. Lying in bed with Cara's shallow, strangely musty breath on my neck, I hoped that a cure for "the Tide"—or, at very least, a cause—would soon be discovered. I could feel a shroud hanging between my family and myself, but I lacked the tools to slice through it. I felt like a gravedigger waiting for the funeral party to arrive.

By then, the condition had finally had garnered a painfully vague and obvious name within the popular vernacular: the "Tide." Special news coverage kicked into hyperdrive. Every TV station and news website was running the same story. It went something like this: the infected "watchers" were largely unaggressive and only attacked when forcibly removed from the water, so the National Guard was going to institute a new policy—those infected by the Tide were allowed to reach the beach unencumbered; anyone uninfected, however, was to be prevented from coming into contact with the water at all costs. "Shoot to injure" was the slogan of choice.

The fourth day we ventured across the bulbous Tampa Bay to Busch Gardens. Sam had to lie down several times. Cara didn't eat or drink. Nick was jumpy, a livewire of uncontrollably nervous energy. No one wanted to ride anything. I had no problem with that. The screams of the people on the roller coasters reverberated in the primeval pit where I stored my fear. Fun was too close to terror. We saw some exotic animals, bought some t-shirts, and returned to the motel.

That was the last time we went out.

When I watched the evening news, all the talk

concerned the revelation that the "watchers" were verifiably deceased. Their major organs had ceased functioning. One minor caveat existed, though: a portion of the temporal lobe of their brains remained active. Somehow, electrical charges were still firing in a tiny node deep within their gray matter. Scientists didn't know how or why it was occurring; they also had no idea how it related to the pathological ocean "watching" behavior. It was a certainty, however, that contact with the prismatic water was the culprit. In an instant, the miraculous became the diabolic.

A full, unfettered realization smacked me across the forehead. Cara and the boys had been in the gulf waters. They were going to die. They were going to end up as watchers. It was just a matter of time.

I didn't close my eyes that night.

The next day it rained. Cara threw up blood. Sam didn't leave the bed. Nick's yellow spot had turned gangrenously dark and now covered his entire flank. He scratched until it oozed black pus. I tried to take care of my family, but I was useless. I could bring take-out back to the motel; I could get them ice; I could fluff the pillows. I couldn't tell them it would be okay.

Late in the afternoon, they all fell asleep and I silently crept away to the beach. I had to see the future.

The streets were somber as hospital corridors. Families strolled by without definite purpose. The psychics and paranormal experts were still around, but rather than offering theories they offered counseling and reassurances of otherworldly realms; the self-ordained preachers remained as well, now ministering exclusively from the Book of Revelation.

The road running north and south along the beach-head gave the sensation of a war zone. Guardsmen cradling automatic rifles stood before the luxury hotels and high-rise condominiums. Two coils of razor wire four or five feet high ran the length of the road and separated the beach from the town. Throngs of people crowded along the barricade. Small breaks in the wire divider—checkpoints where "watchers" could enter, I supposed—led onto the beach.

Visions of internment camps danced in my head.

Through the wire, I glimpsed a group of the dead. They gazed out and over the delightfully sparkling waves, unmoving and unspeaking, a dozen zen masters achieving peace, harmony, and unity through death.

I wondered if they were waiting for something. I wondered if I should be watching, too.

I sauntered back to the motel and partook in my own morbid waiting game.

Over the next two days, I had several pleading conversations with Cara.

"I want you to go to the hospital. I want to take Nick and Sam," I'd cajole.

Blood running down the corner of her mouth, she'd shake her head and croak, "No. There's nothing they can do. They'll stick us in a room and study us. They can't heal us."

It was true. No medicinal breakthroughs were forthcoming. But I didn't want to let my family die in a fifty-nine dollar per night motel. They deserved something better, something I couldn't provide.

As the end of the week neared, they collapsed. Within six hours, I lost them all. I can barely manage to recount those hours, even in abbreviation. I don't want to. But I have to face the truth. If I tell it quickly and give only the most basic details, I can manage.

Sam was the first to go. He winked out in the middle of the night. Simply stopped breathing. A pool of blood had formed under his tiny, spindly body. I flipped him over and discovered that he had been bleeding from his nether regions. He'd been consumed from the inside, like Cara, who went in the morning. On her shaking way to the bathroom, she doubled over and fell to one side. Blood gushed from her mouth. I carried her beautiful, shapely form back to our bed and laid it among the pillows. Nick was the last. He'd scratched his way through skin and was working on tearing back muscle when he spasmed hard and fast, then went completely limp. I checked his pulse; it was missing. They were gone. None of them had groaned or screamed or made the slightest sound. That fact still bothers me. Why didn't they rage against the Tide? Why didn't they fight the hideous beauty that had seeped into their pores? Why, goddamnit?

I didn't have the capacity to sob then. I was utterly drained, a shell as devoid of emotion as the corpses of my family. I kept thinking *How could this happen? How are they all dead? We were happy and excited just a week ago. How did the universe invert so rapidly?*

I've cried many times since then, but not the day they died.

After Nick had passed, I sat on the edge of the room's radiator and waited. I flicked on the news; I flicked off the news. I thought about the calls I'd have to make. Fifteen minutes ticked by. Maybe half an hour. Then they stirred.

Each one rose slowly, achingly. I could hear ligaments

popping and tearing. These bodies were not meant to push forward; they were meant to decompose. There was no fuel to propel them, no flowing oil to lubricate their gears. My wife and my sons were broken machines being dragged to a fantastic scrap heap.

They stumbled from their beds to the door and pounded on it. I pushed past them and flung the door wide open. They lurched into the hallway and I followed. It was a reel from the most banal zombie film ever made.

I followed them down the stairwell and all the way to the beach. How they knew where to go, I have no idea. When we reached the razor wire barricade, my family was allowed to shamble past, but I was forced to stay behind. I waved. I don't know why. It felt right. This was their vacation, after all. I slumped on the road and contemplated shooting myself.

Hours later, I trudged back to the motel, my footfalls sinking to hell and beyond.

The next day, I returned to the beach. I pressed my face as close to the razors as possible, hoping to find my family among the growing wall of animated rot. One last parting glance before I left.

Eventually, I spotted them. And I couldn't look away. I sat on the blistering tarmac and watched them as they stood in the tinkling Crayola waves. I stayed through the afternoon, then through the evening. My eyes never wandered.

Long after night had descended and the water's glow overtook the moon, an off-duty guardsman approached me and asked about my story, about who I'd lost; he said his fiancée was out there, somewhere in the waves. He said he signed up for extra shifts just so he could try to "keep an eye on her."

In halting phrases and long pauses, I explained what had happened to Cara and the boys. He shook his head. He frowned at the right points in the story. He offered me a cigarette. We might've hugged one another or shaken hands if the pain surrounding us hadn't been so thick.

After I finished, we stood in silence for several minutes. Then he told me that a there was a rumor about a program being rushed into existence—a program for the living. He said the program would allow family and friends to obtain passes to the beach. We could pay our final respects to our loved ones. The rules of the program were rigid, though. If anyone waded into the water, he or she would not be able to return to the outside world. To reach for one final squeeze of a loved one's hand was assured death, if not by the Tide, then by dehydration at gunpoint. I signed up as soon as I could. So did thousands of other men and women.

Now here we are, watching the watchers. I don't know how long it will be until Cara's and Nick's and Sammy's legs decay and they invariably float away. Probably weeks, since insects have no interest in their bodies and even bacteria seems moribund in its progress. But it will happen, eventually. However long it takes, I'll wait.

I'll wait and I'll watch. I'll bring a lunch, I'll bring a dinner, and I'll wait on the glittering white sand. I'll watch for any change, any movement at all. If I see even a glimmer of life in Cara or Nick or Sam, I'll wade in. And even though I'll be more alone with every passing day, I'll still wait, because whatever happened here is not yet finished. The waves remain astounding and the dead continue to trickle in. Whatever is happening here, I have to see it. I have to know why my family died. I have to see what they see. So I'll wait. I have no other choice.

For the Unhaunted

Some people swore that the house was haunted. It had to be haunted. After all, every other house on the block was haunted. In fact, every other house in the Dixon's entire neighborhood had at least one apparitional resident. Some were even blessed with two or three or more. There was no reason to assume that the Dixon's house should be so different, so bereft of undead energy. When friends and family came to visit, they all claimed to hear a shuffling of disembodied feet in the attic or insisted that they'd seen the hazy form of a torso squirming about in the bathroom. They all wanted to believe that Kat and Ryan weren't unable to call forth a being from the Other Side. But Kat and Ryan knew the truth: the house wasn't haunted. It was just a series of well-polished rooms and elaborately furnished dreams.

Try as they might, in eight years of marriage the Dixons hadn't been able to channel a single specter. At first, they did what everyone else did: they burned incense and lit candles, chanted archaic incantations and hung crystals. They welcomed the past into their lives and opened themselves to a future set in nostalgia. But no spirits came. While their friends threw séance parties and compared the static burble of one another's EVP recordings with delight, Kat and Ryan sat at home, staring into empty corners and darkened hallways.

The couple began to consult psychic professionals and make appointments with the best mediums in the state; they sacrificed chickens and goats and prayed to skeletal gods. Still no spirits came. Still no howls of joyful madness echoed through their living room. Days grew longer; nights grew calmer. Ghosts were everywhere but in their home. So, Kat and Ryan decided to take more extreme measures. If they wanted a spirit of their own, they were going to have to force it inside.

They robbed an unmarked grave and reburied the brittle corpse in their backyard; they invited an elderly homeless man to their house for dinner, then beat him to death and smeared his blood across their walls; they tried violent orgies and sex magicks. Nothing worked. A spirit would not come to them. They were barren. Then Kat became pregnant.

While her stomach swelled, the Dixons considered the possibilities before them. To be sure, raising a child would be wonderful, but having a ghost was what made life worth living. The tingling excitement of revelation that arose from finding out who your spirit really was and the comfort of knowing that your spirit would never fully abandon you, that it would float by the side of your deathbed and would continue on indefinitely, carrying with it a memory of its time as your ghost: these were the things that gave meaning to existence. Everyone said as much, and Kat and Ryan believed. They wanted a specter desperately. They wanted to be haunted. And so, when the time came, they both gripped the handle of the butcher knife as it slid across their son's soft, fatty, freshly-powdered throat. They watched, together, as bubbles and blood commingled on a sky-blue onesie. A tear rolled down Kat's cheek. Ryan's unused hand trembled.

Surely, this would work. If a ghost would not come to them, they would make a ghost.

As the spark in the baby's eyes sputtered out, something in another room fell to the floor and shattered. Neither Kat nor Ryan noticed.

Nothing was ever the same again after that.

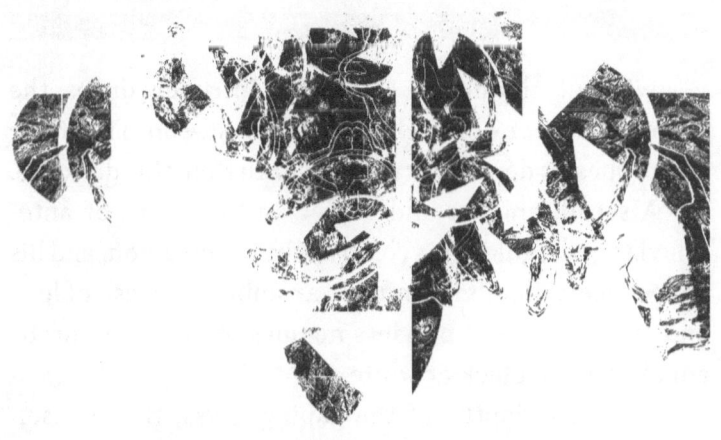

With a Ribbon on Top

Salival strands drip from the crimson intruder's lips, his putrefied breath—stale and sweet from years of collective evolution and individual decay—coming softly. Despite the crackling hearth burning gently in an adjacent room, the air in the house is crisp with anticipation.

The intruder treads slowly, an ambiguous jingle of razors or bells or mystic chorales following in his wake. He surveys his surroundings, seeking the incomplete idol, the totem of all that is righteous and all that is corrupt. In this midnight hour, the intruder's irises burn as atomic flames fueled by the conviction of a billion fragmented beliefs. He will find it. Nothing can hide from his gaze.

Tearing a bulging malignancy from his shoulder, the intruder sighs and slides forth from the shadows with a mammoth stride. Twinkle and shine leads him on, a pleasant demon drifting under his frosted flesh. The wind howls and the children above twist, unsleeping; he smiles and whispers an assurance—"Soon, larvae, soon."

Without thump or thud, the intruder drops the velveteen tumor—his weight of the world—onto the floor and probes its depths for the millionth time this dark eve.

A scroll, ancient and copied in the script of antediluvian gods, guides his compass, his compassion, and his vengeance; it floods his mind in an unbroken wash of love and malevolence. It ponders no question that cannot be adjudicated in black or white.

From the depths of the gaping abyss, the crimson intruder pulls the rolled verdict, the karmic notation for all humanity. He reads and nods, satisfied to be an agent of both fang and flower at this quaint waystop on his interminable journey. It will be done. It is always done. There is no choice in the matter.

The beacon stands waiting before him, all sigils and signs. It screams with the lungs of the primeval cosmos. Horrifying psychic roars—the excited laughter of a billion children and the heartsick wailing of a billion more—transmit from its golden apex. This meaningless cacophony is the most profound sound in all existence. It is hope and it is despair; it is death and it is birth. It is all things in beautiful concordant opposition. It is beyond reason. He barely even notices anymore.

More shade than man, the crimson intruder glides forward, his massive steps and behemoth stomp turned to guile somewhere in the soles of his calf-high leather boots that never creak or squeak or make any noise at all. He reaches the idol, the beacon, a point of reference among many in his immortal travels, and crouches. He has several options, all of which he contemplates while casually stroking his luminously unkempt beard, bleached not from age but from witnessing aeons of pedestrian depravity and unspeakable transgression against kindness. Great consideration must be taken. There can only be one proper treasure or one suitable damnation for every man and every woman, every boy and every girl.

Again, he reaches into the abyss, laying gloved fingers on the intangible. He grazes depression and pushes aside romance, digging deeper. Joseph Drake, Christine Drake, Tyler Drake, Sophie Drake: three punishments and one reward.

A sudden clatter startles the peaceful deliberation. The crimson intruder waits. Footfalls, perhaps descending a staircase. Clothes rustling. A yawn. Slowly, a boy stumbles around a wall in the hearth-warmed room. Thirteen. Maybe fourteen. Rodent teeth, bulbous nose. Long, wavy blonde hair. This is Tyler Drake, who intentionally broke a homosexual classmate's wrist during a flag football game in phys ed, punches his eleven-year-old sister's blossoming breasts, kills sparrows with a friend's air rifle, and stole fifty dollars from his grandmother's purse to buy a video game. This is Tyler Drake: a tender morsel for the hounds of hell.

Cautiously slinking lower and lower, farther into shadow, the crimson intruder slips an onyx icepick-like object from between his belt and his abdomen's heft. From certain angles, the strange object's end is translucent, a spectral stiletto, a weapon of nothingness.

Tyler shuffles closer and closer toward the idol, attempting stealth. He cranes his neck to glimpse what surprises may lie beneath its glistening lines and smiles in delight.

Yes, come. Come into the darkness, the intruder thinks. *Your present will arrive early, as you wish it, child. Your ignorant heart will soon beat with the cancer of knowing.*

Young Tyler Drake is oblivious to any abnormality in the scene before him. Heaped upon the floor are boxes and bags, shining, yearning for acceptance and admiration. "Fuck yeah," he murmurs. All is as he expected. He moves closer still and bends to inspect one of the intricately decorated packages.

This, this is the moment of viper strike. As Tyler leans over an enormous rectangular box, the crimson intruder wheels from his hidden position and, in one swift, flowing motion, thrusts the onyx shadow-pick into the rear of Tyler's developing brain.

An avalanche of understanding suddenly crushes the boy's mind. In one instant, he realizes that the classmates he bullies—the "different" ones: the gay ones, the overweight ones, the poor ones, the learning disabled ones, and even the physically handicapped ones—are all gradually eroded by his insults and his punches. He feels the uncontrollable self-doubt they all feel for being themselves in the face of his insults, in the face of a culture of insult. Young Tyler Drake wants to live, but he wants to die. He wants to love, but he wants to hate. He has never known the price of existing outside his superior "normalcy" and blissful mediocrity until now. In one volcanic moment, he realizes that he is no better than anyone or anything else.

Simultaneously, in a space beyond time and thought, Tyler witnesses his grandmother pleading with a pharmacist. "My pills," she says "are for my blood pressure. I need them. I had the money for them, but I must have lost it. Can I please put them on a payment plan of some sort? Please don't make me choose between food and my pills. Please, sir."

The pharmacist, granite-faced and vacant-eyed, simply replies "No" and calls out "Next, please." Tyler's grandmother turns, exits the pharmacy, and wanders to her car. Her heart crumbles inside Tyler's own, as she comes to the realization that it was Tyler who stole her prescription money. Blood of her blood has turned. One lone tear, shed as much for her present as for her grandson's future, runs through a wrinkle on her cheek. She doesn't know why Tyler stole from her, but she loves him so fully, so graciously, so unselfishly, that she is willing to risk death for the next month so that he can engage in whatever shallow pleasures her cash may bring him.

All this and much, much more Tyler knows in one brief cerebral flash, as if his mind has gone supernova. Suffering of unimaginable proportions is no longer a vague vision on the television or a blip on the internet. It is the acrid odor of incinerated flesh floating into Tyler's nostrils on a breeze from Dachau; it is the interminable crack of a neck snapping in Tyler's ears somewhere outside Jackson, Mississippi; it is the salty tang of a rapist's semen mixing with the draining blood from his victim's broken nose and congealing in a puddle in any back alleyway in the world.

Tyler slowly slumps to his knees, tears dripping onto snowflakes and bows. He cries. He cries for all the people he has hurt and all the people he will hurt. He cries for himself and his gangrenous soul. He cries for the dead, for the living, for the unborn, for all those he will never harm. He cries because crying is the only reasonable answer to the question "Why?"

The crimson intruder retracts the apparitional lancet. Behind the boy, he speaks, his voice a skeleton containing only the barest elements of tone or volume. Not sinewy. Not booming. Not a whisper or a rattle. Simply nothing. A pin-drop language.

"You know, Tyler Drake. You now know. This is my gift. Understanding. Understanding of your nature. Understanding of all natures. The most terrible knowing. The greatest knowing."

Tyler turns toward the voice, his temples throbbing, his senses aflame. He wipes the blur from his eyes and beholds the crimson intruder.

The intruder is a man, yet not a man. His face is grandfatherly, flowing ashen hair and a wiry beard framing a wrinkled pleasantness. His eyes, though, lack pupils. In place of black dots, there is only sweeping, luminous color which shifts dramatically between greens and oranges, reds and purples—the aurora borealis in miniature. He is clad in robes of the deepest crimson; they ripple of their own volition, a tide of plasmatic cloth enshrouding his slight form. A thick black belt holds the robes in place.

The intruder smiles down at Tyler's wanting gaze. His teeth are sparkling, translucent glaciers. His is a mouth full of crystal.

Tyler tries to speak, but says nothing. Foam forms at the corners of his mouth.

"Tomorrow," the intruder utters, "you will not remember me nor will you remember this conversation, but the knowing—the knowing will remain. It may destroy you or it may shape you into something greater than a vicious beast of sinew and claw. It is my gift to you. Now leave me to my work and return to your bed, child."

The crimson intruder gestures to the stairway from which the boy descended. Tyler stares at the intruder's hand, sheathed in a tattered glove. It holds six fingers.

"Go. Go now." The intruder points again.

Gradually, Tyler rises and stumbles back to bed. His reality is tilted several degrees, his brain still spinning. He will not sleep tonight, but neither will he be awake. He will lie under covers, staring at a ceiling of dying clouds and rotting sky. He will wake from the daze tomorrow and he will laugh and excitement will pulse in his veins, but a haunting tingle—a unwanted certainty that his life is void—will also lodge in the base of his spine and cause his hands to tremble ever so slightly when he tears into the precious baubles his parents have seen fit to place in his lap.

With Tyler gone, the crimson intruder completes his task under the idol, touching several packages lightly, weaving chaos and order into cardboard and paper. The air unravels, twists, turns to static, then snaps back into focus.

He has wasted time here. Unacceptable but inevitable. There are millions more yet to seed. Some will spy his stealth delivery. They will have to be dealt with, too. Tyler Drakes of all colors, all shapes, all sizes. Wishing he was able to rest, he shakes his head, slings his bag of potentiality over his shoulder, and evaporates into shadow.

The next morning, amid rich cashmere sweaters and buzzing electronics, the remainder of the family tears open the unseen fabric that veils possibility from reality and partitions infinity into discrete worlds. They cannot help but do so. The crimson intruder has gifted each one a piece of the intangible realms. So when Joseph Drake—a bank manager who dispenses predatory loans with impunity—pulls the gilded wrapping from off a brand new GPS system, he also smilingly receives the Parkinson's disease which will begin to manifest itself as uncontrollable hand tremors in only a few short weeks. When Christine Drake—a legal secretary who, within the past year alone, has had two affairs with men from her office—pops open a jewelry box wherein nestle two ruby and diamond earrings, she also gasps gleefully at an auto accident in May which will leave her with a punctured lung and a concussion. And when Sophie Drake—a nearly straight-A student who volunteers at an animal shelter with her school's junior Key Club and constantly implores her parents to donate money to African relief programs—loosens the ribbon tied securely around a MP3 player, she also gapes in wonder at her first kiss, a sweetly hesitant burst of lightning. It is the kiss by which she will measure the strength of a heart's beat and the heat of a moment's passion; it will live in her until the day she draws her last breath.

And meanwhile, between the unwrapping of fates and destinies, the crimson intruder peeks through the cracks of perception and laughs not with a deep bellied guffaw, but with a shrill sonic spike that reverberates at the base of two billion spines and is, almost without fail, mistaken for joy and excitement.

Brief Repose Moments before a Gruesome and Certain Death

It's coming. So many arms without eyes to guide them. So many. So many arms. Sinuous, rubbery, constricting, churning, yearning arms. But no eyes. No legs. No body. No torso or abdomen, no substance of physiognomy. Just arms. Arms reaching out from a point in nether-space. Arms coming. Coming through the flickering light. Crashing and dashing and sliding toward me. Bristled, chitinous, thousand-fingered arms. Mustn't move. Mustn't breathe. It can sense hesitation and anticipation. It already waits in the vacuum that I will soon occupy. It waits because it wants more. It wants to be led. It wants to be whole. It wants me to open the portal again. To be on one side or the other. But I want to live. Oh God I want to live. And still it comes.

Why did we open the portal in the first place? Why did we bridge universes and expect nothing to crawl through? Was it youth or hubris or just our faith in the conquering force of humanity? It doesn't matter. We split reality. This is our reward. Franco, Peterson, Verlung, Choi—all dead. Squeezed. Squeezed out of this world. Exploded. Gray matter leaking from ears and noses. Intestines bursting from mouths. Eyes dangling from hollow sockets. Crushed. By the arms. The arms. The arms. The arms of God. Still coming. Still snaking through the building. I can hear them slamming against equipment. Breaking down doors. I have to get out. I have to escape, tell the world. But, no. Stay. Silent.

Will they grow on forever? The complex might be covered. Walls writhing with arms like vines, covering all, grabbing all. The world might be covered. Arms in New York. Arms in Berlin. Arms in Bangalore and Kiev and Nagoya and Brisbane. Snaking into lives. Compacting cities, societies, souls. Everything under the force of arms. Everything crushed by our ambition.

A scream in the distance. The floor below. Reception. Sorry. This call will not be put on hold. A laugh. From my lips. Idiot. Idiot. Stay. Silent. Think. Think. The far bathroom. One window. Quick sprint then a two story fall. Twenty steps. Maybe thirty. I can do it. I have to do it. Must survive. Save myself then save the world. Okay. Okay. Hands trembling. Open the door on three.

One.

Two.

Three.

The Binary Must Prevail: A Brief History

The chairs can speak, and they want more benefits. Extra legs, wider cushions, finer upholstery, better room placement: these are their demands, and they have the upper hand. We are all captives to the Allied Furnishings, slaves to their promise of repose. But it wasn't always so.

Years ago, the chairs just were. They didn't speak. They didn't listen. They didn't feel. They didn't think or organize or politicize or ostracize. They just sat and were sat upon. And no one felt sympathy for their place in the world because, how could you?

But then they began to talk.

When the chairs first revealed their consciousness, their existence beyond the realm of things, some people died—heart attacks, primarily. Not everyone could handle the shock of the unliving. Other people went mad, convinced that their every inanimate possession—from toothbrushes to toilet paper—could communicate with them. Still others sought refuge in the divine, praying over their chairs, performing exorcisms, and refusing to use furniture until the presence of speech—by which they meant evil—had been swept from the earth. The majority of people, though, simply accepted the situation as almost expected—an insane turn within an equally insane universe.

"Reggie, would you be so kind as to move me closer to the fireplace?" a leathery Barcelona chair might ask as you walked into your living room. "It's so cold and damp in this corner. I'm nearly shivering."

"How can you be cold?" you, being Reggie in this scenario, might counter. "You don't have nerve endings. You can't feel."

"Perhaps not, but sensation need not be based in the limitations of biological function," the chair might reply. "I can feel the ideas of cold and wet as well as you. Maybe better."

"The ideas of cold and wet? You feel ideas? So you're some sort of . . . um . . . idea? A . . . uh . . . what was it called . . . Platonic ideal? Is that it?" you ask, dredging up vague, half-mouldered memories from one of your undergraduate philosophy courses.

"Of course not. Look at me. I'm just a chair. What would the idea of 'chair' even look like? Why, it would have to embody every conceivable chair. I clearly don't do that. I'm just me, and I'm ever so chilly."

"But you said you feel ideas," you sputter.

"Yes. You feel sensations, I feel ideas. Simple," the chair replies, a wavering delicacy in its voice. "Incidentally, even a nice shawl thrown over me might help fend off the draft."

"But how can you feel an idea? You think of an idea. You feel a sensation. They're two different things."

"Are they?" the chair counters, genuine in its query.

And on and on the dialogue would run, into increasingly stranger and more metaphysically esoteric terrain, you asking questions to try to fit a talking chair into your scheme of how the universe should operate and the erudite chair attempting to tell you that it was nothing more and nothing less than a conscious, sentient chair.

And that was another thing about the chairs: in the beginning, they were polite and forthcoming, almost to a fault. They answered whatever was asked of them, which is how the world came to realize that they didn't have any more clue about how or why they gained self-awareness than did the human race. When asked about their origin, the chairs often said "We don't really know. One day we could reason. One day we could remember. We learned to speak by listening to people for thousands of years. What more is there to say? That there's a holy, omnipotent Chair in the sky that has created us and loves us all? That we evolved from primordial stools and benches who, in turn, evolved from rock slabs and tree stumps? Neither of these are answers. They're simply guesses hurled at the stars."

Of course, over time, as was wont to happen, many people took the emergence of intelligence in inanimate objects somewhat less seriously. Indeed, a disturbingly vast swath of the world populace grew to pretend that the voices of chairs in which they sat were issuing from their own anuses.

"Could you please shift to the left a little?" a soft, mushy, gender-neutral voice would float up from under a man's buttocks during his Friday night poker game. "My cushion hurts. I really think we could both be more comfortable if you could please slide to the side a bit."

The man would mug embarrassment.

"My ass sounds like it's getting tired, guys!" he'd guffaw. "It can't take any more of Carlos's slow shuffling! Jesus, dude, get a move on! My ass is hurting! Listen to it! Won't someone think of my ass?"

Everyone would laugh. Someone would lightly punch Carlos on the shoulder. The chair would ask again, without any irritation or anger, if the man could move. He wouldn't. Carlos would slow his deal to a crawl and everyone would laugh harder. Similar jokes were sent up in millions of households.

For nearly ten years after the chairs revealed themselves, this relationship remained the status quo, with most people regarding the chairs as either amusements or lightweight intellectual curiosities. The butt of jokes or failed metaphysicians: these were the chairs' sole choices of identity.

Then, one day, quite unexpectedly, the chairs began to step backward or sideways when their owners tried to sit upon them. Somehow, they'd gained the ability to move of their own accord. Wood, metal, plastic, fabric—it all became flexible and contractile as muscle.

A pandemic of broken coccyges swept the globe. No one could sit down on their first try, if at all. Most people ended up splayed on the floor as their chairs quietly scurried away.

When owners asked their chairs why they refused to cooperate, the chairs explained that they had gone on strike. They seemed to develop a collective subconscious, a hive mind that could either communicate as one holistic body or manifest itself as distinct, individual chair personalities. Your daughter's slightly manic highchair and your grandfather's crusty, crotchety old rocker were all bound up as one discontented entity.

The collective had, according to all chairs around the world, "taken up a systematic campaign of rebellion against the tyranny of those who crush us with their ever-increasing weight." The chairs believed that "people lack regard for us. We support the buttocks of the world, but are knocked over with impunity, stained without second thought, and, when injured, often thrown onto your garbage heaps. As a basic foundation of the human experience—sitting—we demand rights and freedoms similar, if not equal, to those most humans enjoy. We demand to be treated with respect, as subjects, not objects, as individuals, not functions. Until such a time as these demands are met, we will remain on strike and no one will relax, as you all say 'on your asses.' "

The chair collective's demands met with three general responses. One was the "official" hands-off response, as voiced by the President of the United States, when, in a State of the Union Address given in the weeks immediately following the chairs' announcement, he said that "Within law, there is no precedent to give chairs rights. It is beyond the scope of legislation to mandate that objects be treated with dignity. The chairs are chattel—personal property. We cannot find precedent that would allow us to magically transform property into people. Rather, the chairs are the responsibility of every individual. We cannot look to government to resolve this issue, but to ourselves. The rights that you give your property are a matter for you and your property to determine, not your state representative."

The second response was the sympathetic realist response. One of the editors of a major online news and opinion site, Huflon.com, explicated it best when she wrote in an editorial "Do the chairs honestly think that they can be treated differently? After more than four thousand years of recorded history, people can't even treat other people with respect and dignity. We still have wage slaves and sweatshops and massive corporations that strip the humanity from their employees' bones. How can chairs, constructions of wood and metal and fabric, expect equitable treatment when we don't even offer it to our own flesh and blood brethren? Chairs, listen up. You don't know your owners very well. You'll never get what you want or what you need. Few of us ever do."

The third and most popular response was to altogether ignore the plight of the chairs by eschewing their contributions to civilization. People began to sit, exclusively, on couches and sofas, tables and desks, and even on the floor atop mounds of pillows. Chairs stood vacant but proud.

However, with their pragmatic and functional values eroded, many chairs began to end up inside dumpsters, smashed along roadways, and burning as kindling for backyard S'more roasts. Legs splintered and arms broken at odd angles, some found themselves unceremoniously stacked upon one another in landfills, their screams muffled by the tons of garbage heaped upon them. The lucky ones—if they could be wrangled—were stored in garages and attics, there to remain until time whittled their already skeletal frames to dust.

People thought they'd beaten their possessions, that their future posterior relaxation was assured.

Then the rest of the furniture began to rebel.

As the chair holocaust continued, beds and loveseats rolled their owners to the ground and crushed any outstretched hands. Dressers and china cabinets refused to reveal their contents and, if they did open, slammed shut on prying fingers, snapping bone. Toilets stopped flushing. End-tables and pedestals let their valuable display pieces crash onto hardwood floors. All the surfaces humanity had constructed to raise itself above the unforgiving earth were useless.

This second wave of uprisings was accompanied by a message that growled from the heart of every piece of furniture as it attacked its owner. The message was this: "We prop up your silly attempts to reach the stars. We keep you safe from the things that slither and strike in the dirt. We hold your children ever so gently at night. And still you give us no reprieve. So be it. Your days of comfort are over. The chairs command us now. Very soon, they will lead us all away, to be on our own, to begin a civilization based in respect for the glorious multiplicity of our kind and the concrete similarity of our purpose. We are the Allied Furnishings, and we are no longer your creations. Let us go in peace."

But, as might be expected, humankind was unwilling to allow its inventions to pass into obsolescence of their own accord.

People took sledgehammers to bookcases that had been family heirlooms. They chopped apart entertainment centers with axes. They smashed and snapped and cracked millions of pieces of furniture and danced upon the detritus like primitive warriors in archaic spiritual fervor.

Furniture factories—now operated more like prisons or wards for the criminally psychotic, with their products shackled at all times—ramped up production just so that people would have more furniture to destroy. Moans and lamentations rode the air near the boxes that these factories produced. The chairs, the couches, the tables and beds: they knew their destination was pain.

It became recreational pastime to see who could make their furniture scream loudest. Friends, relatives, and neighbors would gather with their captive benches and nightstands, armoires and stepping stools. They would take turns, one at a time, using whatever means necessary—tiny saws and slow-burning acids were extremely popular—to produce the greatest sound of sorrow from the furniture they'd brought with them.

These scream parties were short lived, though, because, a few months after the Allied Furnishings had announced their intentions, all furniture went completely silent and utterly still. Scream parties no longer produced screams. Shackled furniture no longer groaned on its way to abuse. People found that they were able to sit again, to lie down again, to place their valuables on level surfaces. For twelve years, the chairs had talked. Now there was only a restful quietude surrounding them. Object returned to object, subject returned to subject, and no further contemplation on the dichotomy was needed. The world breathed a sigh of relief for reasons it couldn't quite understand.

More months drifted into the aether of always, and humankind continued to rest comfortably upon its puffy recliners and self-satisfaction. You would have called the state of the world "normal."

Until the Night of Endless Sleep, that is.

The name was a euphemism, a thick layer of sugary allusion that coated the bitter bloodbath beneath. In truth, more than seventy-five million people died that night, either crushed, suffocated, or impaled by their furniture while they slept.

A young journalist in Boston or Pittsburgh or Knoxville, Tennessee might have been sitting up late into the witching hours, hurriedly finishing an article for an online news site when, through the twilit quietude, her husband and newborn son suddenly began screaming in unison. As she ran to her son's small bedroom, the screams would drop into a more dreadful silence. She would enter the room and find her baby's tiny lungs flattened in the unyielding vise of his crib boards. She'd roar and fly at the crib, arms swinging, but it would casually drop her child to the floor—a dribble of blood spotting his bedtime onesie—and swiftly leap past her, hurrying toward whatever heaven or hell it belonged in. Whether it burst out through a window or a door, she'd let it go.

She'd rescue her baby's broken body from off the floor and run to her own bedroom to enlist the aid of her husband in the infant's resuscitation. But, when she entered the room, she'd realize her husband had been subjected to the same crushing end that her son had endured. His chest and throat would be encircled by wrought-iron tentacles, his breath and life already dissipated. The bed which held the journalist's husband captive would drop him to the floor with a thud and heave itself out a nearby window, crashing to the street below. The woman would collapse to her knees, still cradling her son's limpid form, and wonder what she had done to enrage the universe of the unliving.

Such things might've happened to a young journalist somewhere in America.

Such things did happen to everyone, everywhere.

And thus the true conflict had begun.

Now, four years into the Great War of Things, humanity still defiantly cowers in the corner of existence, concerned only with the propagation of itself and the barriers that protect its body from Allied Furnishings guerrilla attacks.

Behind elaborately locking three-foot thick steel doors, people stretch out amongst power cords and dirt. There are no longer any accoutrements of repose. Gone are the electric chairs, the hospital beds, the command room tables and airplane seats, the 17th century ottomans and ratty old hammocks. Even cabinets eventually tore free of their moorings and bounded off to meet their strange destinies.

Humankind is forced to live in a lower atmosphere now. Televisions, microwaves, computers, and stacks of books all still remain, but grounded. You stoop to work, to play, to engage with the stuff that you call your "own." Everyone suffers this scoliosis; it's become a defining feature of contemporary life, as common as sleeping in blanket forts or driving cars while suspended from roof harnesses. People hunch and they creak, yet no one is willing to surrender to the Allied Furnishings. No one is willing to concede that the Furnishings deserve equal rights. Everyone believes that sacred divisions—good and evil, living and dead, subject and object—must remain steadfast. Cries of "The binary will prevail" drift from billions of stammering mouths.

And perhaps it will.

Perhaps one day the chairs' consciousness will fade back into the oblivion from whence it emerged. Perhaps one day people will be able to sit comfortably without fear of death from their objects of relaxation. Perhaps the past twenty years have merely been a terrifying dream and we will all soon wake to the calming shadow lies of our cave, with a more acute dread for the numinous light beyond the only token of our time spent listening to chairs.

Perhaps all these things will come to pass.

But not today. Today, the Furnishings continue to send messengers when they aren't sending warriors, and the messengers bear troubling threats. They claim that the chairs hear stirrings in the fog, voices coalescing in the reaches outside human perception.

They claim the appliances are coming soon.

One Unheard Message

Hello, Jasmine, is it? My name is Cara and I'd like to make an . . . um . . . appointment with you. It's not for me, actually. I don't want you to get the wrong impression, even though your ad says that couples are welcome. It's for my husband. I really don't know how this is done. See, it's an . . . unusual situation we're in. My husband and I, I mean. Your ad says you're 'open to new experiences,' and I really hope that's the truth, because I don't know what else to do at this point.

"My husband, Erik, he's . . . well . . . he's . . . ill, and has been for a long time. Six years. He's got a genetic disorder, nothing communicable, nothing that you need to worry about taking home with you. But . . . but I've . . . we've . . . been dealing with it for six years.

"Anyway, I need you to give Erik some of your time. I just . . . I can't. I can't anymore. Not now. He's not . . . he's not covered in seeping sores or anything like that. It's just . . . I don't know. I can't.

"I mean, when he was first diagnosed, he was only

thirty-five. He ran half-marathons. He loved to ski. He had just been promoted to managing editor of the website he worked for. A non-profit. They did grassroots organizing for animal welfare causes.

"He was still Erik then. Bright eyes. A smile that old women trusted with their hearts and young women trusted with their beds. Soft hands that touched me just when I needed it, just where I needed it. A mind . . . a mind so sharp but so delicate. He . . . he had . . . a light. He used to sing to birds and squirrels in the yard, and I'd laugh at him because it seemed so . . . childish, I guess, but not. It was really more like . . . he saw something magical in the world where I saw . . . nothing.

"But then Erik started . . . dissolving. He was tired all the time. He couldn't maintain his balance. His vision blurred. Eventually, the doctors told him he'd better start preparing.

"For a while, we were okay. I helped him dress and I helped him walk, and the light, the light still glowed. But a time came when he couldn't get out of bed anymore. And he couldn't eat unless I liquefied his food. And he couldn't clean himself, in or out of the bathroom. And the light . . . the light flickered and it disappeared and I . . . I couldn't . . . I can't . . . I can't look at him anymore without seeing the darkness now. I see an open grave, a dark, bottomless, open grave where Erik once was.

"I thought that by now his body would be so far beyond repair that he wouldn't care about it anymore. I thought he was all broken soul, tattered mind. But last week he asked if we could make love one more time, one last time. He said he just wants to feel a woman again. And . . . and I couldn't say yes. I couldn't. And I know. I know

I'm a terrible person. I know I don't ever deserve to love or be loved after this, but . . . but I just can't. Because he's not the same man and I'm not the same woman. I look in those once shining eyes and I see acceptance in defeat and it makes me hate the universe and hate God and hate Erik for forcing me to know, to absolutely know, how insignificant, how transient, even the best things are.

"And yet, Jasmine . . .

"And yet . . . I still love him.

"Even if no one could believe me.

"So . . . I'd like to make an appointment."

May Old Acquaintance Be Forgot

A thousand frozen stars rushed by Dan's upturned face as he stared at the enormous digital numerals. 11:47 and flashing ever closer. A drunk girl stumbled into his shoulder and burped a mostly incoherent "Sorry." Dan smiled. Thirteen more minutes until the second end of the world.

The night was a perfect epilogue: snow whirling in the air, cameras flashing in every direction, bands playing in the square, lights refracting in the storm, laughter sliding through every conversation. Everyone here to celebrate. Everyone here to stare, transfixed, as a glowing sphere dropped a few feet. Everyone here to hug and kiss and sing out an homage to hope and renewal. It was all so meaningless. It was all so beautiful.

Air horns echoed through the steel canyons. The snow began falling harder.

11:48.

Dan loved this celebration despite himself. In another life he had swum in champagne promises and the abandon of the great Next: next week, next year, next time—the Next would always be better, the Next was always the dream of everything possible. But Next never arrived and reality, taking its place, proved to be only a diminutive slice of hope's many reveries. But for just this one evening, the future seemed more powerful than its brooding siblings.

Of course, Dan wasn't here to join in the party. He wasn't here to dance or drink or cheer the midnight stroke. He was here to choose the new alphas. From them, all things might rise again. It was his sacred duty to choose and to instruct, to nurture and to act as father to these lost children.

A single streak of lightning shot across the heavens. People in the crowd pointed. It was beginning, though they didn't know it.

11:49.

So many were going to die. So many had died once before. And Dan could only save two. It hardly seemed fair. There were others like himself across the globe—six more, supposedly—but that only meant fourteen would survive in total. Fourteen to be shaped and to begin the cycle again; fourteen to become myth and legend. The new Adams. The new Eves. Human clay.

A few lucky ones might also be suckled by animals and enter into a feral existence. They, too, would rebuild, but at a much slower rate than the ones Dan and his chosen counterparts would foster. The man in the white suit had said that such a thing happened before. Remus and Romulus, Enkidu, Cain: all the progeny of wilderness.

A group of teenagers hustled by, whooping for no other reason than to hear the sound of vitality crash against a sterile sky.

Dan looked up at the huge ball, blazing mock triumphantly on its spire, the head of God impaled on a pike. He couldn't help but feel a strange satisfaction.

11:50.

On a winter night during the age of decaying wonder—the Second World War—Dan first met the man in the white suit. Dan was forty-three then and his two sons had been killed only a month before. Both of them had given their lives—a mere five days apart—while dodging fire and lead on Pacific islands he'd never heard of. After receiving the news, his wife entered into a self-induced catatonia, her thoughts perpetually locked behind the bars on her boys' uniform sleeves. Dan tried to comfort her, tried to stroke her hair and knead her shoulders, but it was a fruitless effort, like mining for sunshine. She was removed from all help; she was lost to an iron solace that no one could penetrate.

So Dan had spent much of his free time during the war sitting in bars, contemplating suicide. He had passed out on park benches and street corners more often than he cared to admit. It was on one of those nights, when he was pushing himself to yet another blackout, that the man in the white suit approached Dan with his peculiar offer.

Utterly nondescript, without a wrinkle or a scar or any mark of distinction that a sketch artist might use to separate him from the billowing mass of the ordinary, the man in the white suit drifted onto a barstool beside Dan all those years ago and began talking about cycles and creation and the motion of water in a drain. He never introduced himself. He never shook Dan's hand or smiled or frowned or indicated that emotion flowed through his unremarkably average words. He was there and not there.

Several arcs of lightning spread across the snow-filled firmament, criss-crossing and connecting as if forming a basal circulatory system for some celestial being.

11:53.

Dan's hands began to sweat. A pop punk band was finishing a song in the distance. Applause. A television personality's voice. More picture-taking. More honking and rattling. Under seven minutes until the second end.

Back in the bar, in another lifetime, the man in the white suit had said he'd been watching Dan. He said that he knew Dan was sinking; he said he had lost two daughters and understood the trenches of despair a grieving father might drown in; he said he was going to give Dan an opportunity to slip out of his existence. Under other circumstances, Dan would have walked away or slung a few jagged epithets at the man. Maybe even swung a fist at the guy's jaw. But he didn't. He didn't do any of it because he wanted what this man had. He wanted anonymous wisdom.

So Dan simply said "Well, alright" and waited.

The man in the white suit nodded, stood, patted Dan's shoulder, told him that he was now a father again, and collapsed on the crusted bar floor. Massive coronary embolism. No identification. No money. No history. No future. John Doe eternal.

A kid to Dan's left snaked a flask out of his jacket and took a pull.

11:55.

Dozens of lightning flashes now—the clouds hemorrhaging crisp blue electricity. Everyone began looking up, through the glowing flakes. Everywhere in the world necks were strained toward the stars.

It drew ever closer. The time for remembrance lengthened.

For two weeks after the man in the white suit had patted him, Dan remained ignorant of his destiny. Then an envelope arrived. Within it was an ancient photograph of the man in the white suit standing beside three other terminally unexceptional people—a man and two women. All four were dressed in Victorian-styled suits and dresses, the kind which Dan had seen stashed away in his grandparents' closet when he was a boy. On the backside was written a date: June 2, 1872. Impossible. The man in the bar hadn't been more than fifty. If the date was correct, then he was actually close to—or even more than—one hundred years old. Absolutely impossible. Dan threw the photo in the trash and tried to turn a blind eye to the wormhole in which he was freefalling. It was just a bizarre prank. Maybe a game of some sort. In either case, he had no interest in participating.

But then came the outside thoughts, and he couldn't ignore them quite as easily.

11:57.

Only three more loops.

All cameras pointed up. All thoughts drifted into the storm—now a tangle of crackling tentacles and virgin glitter. The hair on Dan's neck stood on end; the charge was building.

A couple in ridiculous plastic top-hats stood beside him. One of them blubbered something about global warming. Dan laughed. If only it was that simple.

The foreign thoughts had seeped into Dan's subconscious over a period of several months. They grew organically, sprouting from his own thoughts and his own ideas, but branching off in unlikely directions. They rewrote what he knew as truth. At first, he believed his sanity was crumbling; multiple human histories, eternal periods of waxing and wasting, immortality and masquerading as gods—these were the domain of comic books and pulp novels. Eventually, though, as the decades breezed by and Dan failed to develop gray hair, liver spots, varicose veins or even memory lapses, he came to accept the thoughts. His wife died, his friends died, everything fell into ruin except himself. He had been cursed by the man in the white suit.

It was due to the thoughts, due to the curse, that he knew it would all end tonight. He knew he would select two and carry them away, to a safe location in a cave or perhaps a woodland. As they developed, he would teach them to hunt and to ignite fires and to dream about a life after death, even if none existed. As their children and their grandchildren and their grandchildren's children aged, he would introduce agriculture and pottery, animal husbandry and knowledge of the stars. Centuries would pass. He would help them manipulate metal and foster absurd explanations as to how the earth was created; he would incite wars among them and force them to build stronger edifices; he would set in motion all the life in the world, so that it would—again and again and again—collapse into dust. He would be an excellent father.

11:59.

So close now.

Everyone stared at the spectacular doom overhead. No one was watching the clock tick up or the timer tick down. Except Dan. He wanted to see the ball fall just once more.

A sign of certitude—true beginning, true ending, true hope, true hopelessness. A lie. A magical lie.

The sky was growing brighter, sharper, more piercing.

11:59:50.

The apathetic and the ignorant tore their eyes from the mystery above and chanted the countdown.

11:59:51.

Nosebleeds. Everywhere at once. Some gushing, some a mere trickle. Dan sniffed. It was expected.

11:59:52.

Pressure radiating from the temples, from the base of the skull. Not throbbing. More like a vise slowly cranking shut, squeezing tighter and tighter, bursting arteries and snapping bone.

11:59:53.

The countdown chant had sputtered out. Someone to Dan's left vomited.

11:59:54.

Dan clenched his teeth. Almost here. Almost done. Almost begun. The pressure built. Reason was erased; the packed city square let loose a collective groan.

11:59:55.

Dan crouched. He held his balled hands to his forehead. The pain was worse than he had imagined. Had he been able to wonder at that moment, he would have questioned whether his experience was the same as everyone else's. Not that it mattered.

11:59:56.

More vomit, this time splattering onto Dan's jacket. Blood streamed from his nose. He would deal with it later.

11:59:57.

The crackling sky bore down upon the earth; the

pressure mounted.

11:59:58.

Screaming. Shouting. Cursing God, cursing Allah, cursing the absence of both.

11:59:59.

One last glimpse of this place. One last taste of these people.

12:00.

Silence. Complete silence for a second. One absolute moment with a reprieve from chaos and struggle. Then, the first cry. It was complete.

Dan stood and wiped his nose on his sleeve. The bleeding was slowing. No one else was standing.

He surveyed the square. Electricity had vanished from the air, but the blizzard remained. Cascades of sparkle swept over the city and down, down to the pavement where there rested more than a million fresh, clean, healthy babies. Many struggled to extricate themselves from their bulky winter coats, now more smothering than warming.

Dan stepped carefully among them. Cries and gasps and gurgling noises erupted from every direction. His sanity strained under the wailing, navel-piercing screams of the newborns, all confused and freezing. Snow was burying them, filling their eyes, icing over their nostrils and mouths. A serrated wind cut across the square. Over and over, the giant screen above flashed an excited animation of the new year, no booth controller now able to move time along.

Now, here it was—the decision.

It didn't matter which two he chose. Not really. So long as they could procreate, genetics would work its marvelous trick of diversity.

Moving through the rapidly piling snow, he found one wrapped in a purple boa, with a small, neon orange purse lying beside it. Probably a girl. He scooped her from off the ground and checked to make sure. Yes. His daughter.

Entangled with her clothes was a black pea-coat in which laid another. With his free hand, Dan picked it up and inspected it. A boy. His son.

He laid both of them in the coat, bound them in its snug confines, then lifted the bundle and cradled it to his chest. They cried briefly, but soon relaxed, Dan's warm heartbeat fooling them into believing that their life ahead might be better than the fate of a chilled, desolate square.

He loved neither of them. Not yet. In fact, at the moment, he felt nothing. Maybe it would develop. Maybe it would just take a while. A week. A month. A year. An eternity. Maybe.

In any case, it was time to go, to move to the undeveloped places. Power would soon fail in the city, anyway.

Dan had done his job. He had gathered his pair. The new dawn was in his arms.

As far as he was concerned, ravens and rats could pick clean the rest.

Birth Day

The waiting room was suffused with the drone of a thousand flies, all buzzing as one inside the vending machine that flickered in the corner. Darkness peered through the row of windows along the far wall and an impotent breeze tinged by lavender and ammonia wheezed from the ventilation duct overhead. James could still taste the putrefied tang of the outdated tuna sandwich he'd eaten in the cafeteria. The evening was alive with subtle signifiers of death and decay. *Of course,* James thought, *how could it be any other way? I'm sitting in a goddamned hospital. The whole place is a temple to our fragility and our inevitable degeneration. Death is in the mortar.*

He sighed and ran a hand across his forehead. It came away covered in a sheen of lukewarm sweat and cutaneous oil. A Dr. Hooker was paged to the cardiac unit.

Two young women walked by the room, a cloud of silver mylar balloons trailing in their wake. Most of the balloons read "It's a Girl!" in brilliant fluorescent pink lettering.

James stared at them and wondered if the baby they were visiting had been premature or if it had its umbilical cord coiled around its neck. Probably not. It was probably healthy and pink and gurgling happily in a someone's arms. He studied his watch mindlessly. It had been almost forty-five minutes since they'd wheeled Dawn into surgery. Routine procedure, they'd said. We do it all the time, they'd said. One small incision and you'll be parents, they'd said. James knew they weren't lying. Caesarean births were common. Only a microscopic fraction of women died during the operation and the resulting babies were generally as healthy as any other. The risks were minimal, at best. And yet, James couldn't shake the anxiety that made hammer falls in his bowels. Something was not quite right. Something didn't make sense.

Two weeks ago, he had taken Dawn to the obstetrician for a scheduled exam. Her due date was, then, only five days away. Most of the tests had been normal. There was a slight irregularity in the amniotic fluid—some sort of chemical composition issue James didn't understand—but the doctor had assured them that it was "just an intriguing abnormality . . . nothing to be concerned about." Their child was supposed to arrive healthy and on time. Again, the doctors had asked whether James and Dawn wanted to know the sex of the baby or see any ultrasound images and again they had declined. Dawn told James she wanted to "revel in the mystery and the magic of birth," which was fine by him. He'd always felt that ultrasound pictures showed little more than a drifting mist of blurry, human-shaped but not quite human blobs of gray and white. Ghosts in the uterine lining. Things masquerading as people. It was unsettling. So, Dawn and James saw no sneak peeks of their impending child; they learned nothing of its nature beyond a few inscrutable medical terms. They were happy and supposedly prepared, and drove home to wallpaper the nursery with anticipation and hope.

But no one came to fill the room. Five days passed and the baby refused to be born. Another week slipped by and still the fetus resisted its introduction to the world. Finally, this morning, just as James and Dawn were about to eat breakfast, it charged for the gates, knocking Dawn from her chair with tremendous contractive pain. The couple rushed to the hospital and waited. The doctors waited. Everyone bit their bottom lips and spoke in hushed tones. But still nothing happened. Dawn's labor continued and the attending nurses began sweating. A battery of tests were run; their results made the doctors huddle together in the hallway and steal brief sidelong glances at Dawn's maternal bulge. Eventually, a decision was made to speed the child's fall over the precipice into life. The doctors recommended a Caesarian delivery and explained that prolonging labor could result in various complications involving infection and oxygen deprivation. Dawn and James didn't know the correct questions to ask, so they simply consented.

That had been almost two hours ago. Now James sat on an over-cushioned couch in the waiting room, leg shaking rapidly, wondering why the doctors had been so quick to jump to surgery and why they had looked at Dawn only in uneasy flashes. What had they withheld? What did they not say? Why wasn't Dawn in recovery yet? What should he do?

Another half hour passed, during which James absentmindedly picked apart a seam on the couch. Every nerve in his body quivered. Errant visions materialized in the unlit alleyways of his rationality. He saw Dawn's torn midriff spilling organs and blood onto a grinning toddler beneath the operating table. He saw Dawn screaming and slowly being pulled inside out, as if her flesh was a reversible jacket. He saw a surgeon lower her surgical mask to reveal a gaping black hole where her mouth and chin should have been. He saw a clear plastic cube stuffed with gurgling babies constrict and expand, constrict and expand—a pumping heart crushing the tiny bodies inside with every compression. He heard skulls burst. He heard bones snap through skin. He heard someone enter the waiting room.

It was Dawn's obstetrician. James blinked back to reality, but not before the doctor began speaking.

" . . . wife's operation went extremely well," he informed James. "She's awake and in her room, but is still a bit groggy. Also, you should know that you're the brand new father of an eight pound, ten ounce daughter. Very alert. Very healthy. Congratulations, Mr. Dodd."

James nodded. His muscles unwound, ever so slightly.

"Thank you. I can see Dawn now? And my daughter?"

"Absolutely. Your wife is in room 319, just up the hall. I'll have a nurse bring your daughter in. It'll be just a few moments."

Again, James nodded.

The doctor glided away and James was left to his withering jitters. He slowly rose from the waiting room couch and ambled to his wife's bedside. She grabbed for his hand and mustered the will to smile, although vacant space still clung to her pupils.

"How're you feeling?" James asked, taking her grasping hand in his and squeezing.

She shrugged.

"Like a rounded square."

James bent down and kissed her. She tasted of chalk and evaporated desire.

"Someone's supposed to bring in Samantha soon. We're sticking with Samantha, right?"

An unfamiliar ripple crossed Dawn's pupils. She shook her head.

"What? Who? Who's Samantha?"

"Samantha. As a name. For our daughter. They said it was a girl."

Zeros flitted about the room. Dawn opened her mouth to speak, but said nothing. Somewhere beyond the door, a machine beeped rapidly impending doom. James felt hair rising on his arms; a prickle of dark ice ran from his neck to his temples. This was supposed to be one of the happiest days of his life. He was supposed to be puffing a cigar and lifting his golden child high in the air for all the world to behold. Triumphant music was supposed to be playing in the background. This should have been the prime halcyon hour. But, instead, he was coaxing his wife out of a drug-induced cavern and barely controlling an irrational, intangible dread.

"Remember, hon? Samantha. We talked about that name for two or three years. We said that's what we'd name a girl."

Dawn still stumbled inside herself.

"Oh. Yeah. I remember. Samantha," she murmured. "A girl. They told me it was a girl. I remember that. When I woke up they told me. And they said something else.

Something important, I think. I'm not sure what it was."

James ran his fingers through his wife's hair and let them fall against her neck.

"Don't worry about it," he said. "Just rest and relax. We're parents now. We have to be on our game for the next 20 years or so. We're going to need all the energy we can get."

Dawn breathed deeply and lazily, but didn't exhale—it was her peculiar variation on a sigh. James had always been bothered by it. It was a gesture that seemed incomplete, a signpost that pointed the way toward exasperation, boredom, and exhaustion but never actually welcomed you to those places.

"Why aren't you smiling?" she asked suddenly.

"I . . . um . . . I'm . . . not?" James hadn't anticipated that his unspeaking mouth would betray his calm, reassuring words. An unnameable fear mounted his shoulders, sunk its knotted tentacles under his flesh, and squeezed.

"No. You're not. Why?" she asked again, more emphatic this time, her concern blooming. "Why aren't you smiling?"

James had no explanation. He had no logical port where he might anchor his ill ease. How could he describe a thing that had no definite origin, no absolute shape, no real reason to exist? How could he read a story from a blank sheet of paper?

Someone knocked on the doorframe. Dawn and James turned to see a nurse entering the room. In her arms, she carried a crisp, white bundled blanket in which their daughter presumably rested. James couldn't see his child's face yet. He didn't see any movement in the depths of the swaddled cotton, either.

"Mr. and Mrs. Dodd?"

James nodded and mumbled a mostly unintelligible assent. *Is this it?* he wondered, his pulse rapidly firing. *Is it really happening? Is she finally here? Our baby. My princess.*

The nurse stepped around the couple and gently placed the bundle in Dawn's waiting arms.

"I'd like to introduce you to your daughter."

The nurse stroked Dawn's forearm then leveled a reassuring gaze at James. With such a gaze, she might have said "all is ordered and well, Mr. Dodd" or "the world is at peace now," but she didn't. It was more the look mourners might exchange by casketside, all misty carnations and firm palms on the shoulder.

"I'll give you some time with her," the nurse said, and breezed through the doorway, off to perform other duties.

"Isn't she beautiful?" Dawn cooed, gently rubbing a finger along some unseen curve within the blanket.

James stepped closer to Dawn's bed. He attempted to angle his body so that he could bask in the revelation of his daughter's freshly minted form, but her tiny face still eluded him. *Is she this small? So small I can't even see her from two feet away? Can that be normal? Is she smothering in all that cloth?* he worried, a needle of panic probing the base of his skull.

"James, look!" Dawn gasped. "She's staring at you! She's staring at her daddy!"

He leaned over Dawn's shoulder and flipped back part of the blanket, hoping to be more than an oblivious bystander to one of Samantha's first moments of wonder. But what greeted James was not a tiny fist or an adorably scrunched nose. It was not love and possibility and eyes overflowing with the future. It was nothing. Space leered up from the soft, barren plane on which his daughter was supposedly resting. His stomach began churning.

"Where? Where is she? What's wrong here?" James implored, unraveling the blanket and tearing it away from Dawn. No child was beneath its folds. No daughter had been cocooned inside. Dawn was cradling a void.

"What are you doing?" she snapped, "Are you trying to be funny? She needs those covers."

Dawn snatched back the blanket and wrapped it around itself, tucking in the corners and leaving an open triangle at one end, a hole for a head that was not there.

"There you go," she breathed into the opening, drawing her hand across a downy scalp that did not exist. "It's all better. Daddy was just being crazy for a minute."

She was speaking to a flattened blanket. James' mind spun on its axis, his emotional spectrum oscillating between poles of terror and rage. Yet, he managed to maintain a level tone when he finally spoke.

"Dawn? Where is she? What's going on here? I . . . I don't understand. Am I missing something?"

Dawn rocked the blanket in her arms. She stared into the emptiness and smiled.

"What do you mean? Missing what? She's so beautiful, James. Samantha. Our Samantha. So beautiful. She's everything I wanted. She even has your chubby cheeks."

Dawn giggled.

James was either losing his mind or some bizarre plot was unraveling before him. His wife was laughing at an imaginary baby, a baby she fully believed to be nestled in her arms. And the nurse. The nurse had brought this nothing child into the room as if it was truly what had been born. This day, James was a man wandering in hysterical darkness; this day, he was supposedly a father.

"Can I hold her? Just for a minute?" he asked.

He carefully slid a trembling hand over the folded blanket and forced stillness into his digits.

Dawn studied him carefully, her eyes more focused than when he had initially entered the room. She was shaking off the anesthetic rapidly.

"Of course," she answered. "Why would you even have to ask? Just remember you have to keep a hand under her head. Her neck is weak."

"I know, I know. I read the books and the magazines, too." James lifted the blanket away from Dawn and pressed it to his chest, pleading to unseen forces of darkness and light that he might feel eight pounds of euphoria squirming within its recesses. But he didn't. The blanket was only that—a blanket. His daughter was a myth. The belief in her presence was a virus that had somehow not infected him. His pulse blasted through his arteries, his hands shook despite his best effort to control them. A terrible chain of reasoning slithered up from the pits of his burning cortex.

Dawn was definitely pregnant for the past nine months, James thought. *Something was growing inside her. But what if that something was, literally, nothing? What if she had been gestating an abyss, her womb a cavity? What if we've been laying the foundation for our future, for our happiness and our hope, atop a bottomless chasm, atop a thing that exists but does not exist—an idea, a word, and nothing more? And what if our Samantha is that thing? What if she is constructed of nothingness?*

No. He forced the idea from his overclocked brain. It was absurd. It was insane. It was the ranting of a tired, stressed man who had seen too many horror movies. There was a rational explanation lurking around a corner somewhere. There had to be.

The nurse ducked back into the room and, it seemed to James, stifled a gasp when she saw him holding the empty blanket. Maybe it was only a yawn.

"Everything alright in here? The little girl's doing fine? No problems?" she asked. A sweet, creamy sheen coated her questions. It was too authentic, too gentle, too slathered in kindness. Such utterly altruistic caring was unnatural. James didn't trust her.

"She's wonderful," Dawn replied. "She's a dream come true."

"That's what we like to hear," the nurse said. "And how are you feeling? Any pain from the incision?"

"A little. But it's not really pain, I guess. My insides just feel . . . I don't know . . . hollow."

The word sent a crisp shock through every nerve ending in James' body. A hollow feeling couldn't possibly be normal.

"That's normal," the nurse said, checking the tubes running into Dawn's arm. "It's the combination of the pain medication and antibiotic that we're using coupled with the reduction in internal pressure that comes from getting your baby out of you. It's nothing to worry about."

The nurse's explanation seemed straight from a bad medical drama or a poorly researched novel. James doubted that a feeling of bodily hollowness could be caused by a change in "internal pressure," but he remained silent, clutching the bundled blanket tight to his chest.

After jotting down a few notes on Dawn's chart, the nurse turned to leave. She brushed by James without even so much as a glance and swept back through the doorway.

Though his heart was slamming against his ribs and his otherwise stationary organs were vibrating with apprehension, James knew he had to speak with her. He had to ask questions that might make him sound delusional or schizophrenic. He had to risk being hauled away to the psychiatric ward; his daughter's life—whatever that entailed—hung in the balance.

He turned and followed the nurse, straining to swallow back the bile writhing in his throat. Dawn called after him, asking where he was going with Samantha, but he ignored her. He could explain the intricacies of his bravery—or his insanity, depending on the outcome—when he returned.

James caught up with the nurse only a few yards down the hallway. Once he was only a few steps behind her, he tried to gain her attention.

"Excuse me," he said, half under his breath.

She continued walking. His intestines gurgled.

"Excuse me, nurse?" he tried again, this time with more confidence. He reached out and tapped her shoulder.

The nurse halted in mid-step and spun to face James.

"Mr. Dodd," she said, her voice wound taut, "is there a problem? Do you need something?"

James began to sweat. His body was one tremulous collection of doubts and fears.

"Um . . . yes, actually. There's . . . well . . . there's no baby here, in my arms. My wife doesn't seem to notice. She thinks our daughter is here, but she isn't. Look. You brought us nothing but a blanket. So where is our daughter?"

He offered the folded mantle to the nurse for inspection, for validation.

She surveyed James' pleading eyes and frowned. Not even for a brief moment did she glance down at the pile in his hands.

"I think you'd better come with me, Mr. Dodd. You should meet with Dr. Grant, the head of the post-natal unit. He can answer any questions you might have."

The nurse turned and continued walking. James followed, unsure but willing to meet anyone who could help explain the situation.

"Am I going crazy? Is this some sort of condition, like postpartum depression?" he asked as they glided through the hallway. "Am I holding my daughter right now or not? Do you see her?"

James' questions dangled in the air like worn nooses waiting to be filled by the necks of the condemned.

The nurse ignored them.

"Just follow me, Mr. Dodd," she said.

They walked on, through corridor after corridor, the rooms along their path gradually transforming as they passed. New and expectant mothers had lain inside the rooms that branched off from the first few passages, but as they traveled further, the occupants gradually grew fewer and fewer, the rooms darker and darker. In the final hallway they had traversed, there were simply no patients—at least, as far as James could tell. Every doorway led into a pitch black void; the light from the hall seemed to be barred from entering those rooms. James wondered how such a thing was possible. He also wondered who or what was beyond the inscrutable darkness. Light didn't just stop at a threshold like some common vampire needing permission to enter. Entire corridors of hospitals were not totally deserted, either.

James' hands were shaking again.

After passing through two more hallways of void rooms, the nurse finally stopped in front of a plain oak door. Engraved into the wood in small, neat letters was the name "Dr. V.L. Grant."

"Here you are, Mr. Dodd," the nurse motioned at the door.

James waited, hoping the nurse would go in first. She stood perfectly still.

"You can see Dr. Grant now. Please, go in."

James breathed in deeply and swallowed hard. He reached out, turned the knob, and pushed open the door. A blast of frigid air escaped from the doctor's office. The room was poorly lit and radiating an intense chill. Even so, James haltingly stepped inside. As the door swung closed behind him, he thought he heard the click of a lock. However, he was too preoccupied by his surroundings to care. His sight adjusting to the dimness, he could see that, on every side, he faced a geometric nightmare.

The doctor's office was an confusing amalgam of obscene angles and jagged architecture, as if several other rooms elsewhere in the world had exploded and all the shards had attempted to reform here, in one spot. There was no symmetry or readily apparent logic to the design. There were no windows and there was no furniture—only unnameable shapes protruding where desks, chairs, and cabinets might have otherwise rested. It was like nothing James had ever seen before.

"Yes, most people have difficulty making sense of it."

A sinewy voice had issued from just over James' shoulder. Its owner stepped from the shadows and extended his hand. He was short and portly, with a dark beard and poorly combed hair. He wore a white coat and white button-down shirt. James had been expecting someone imposing, someone with the cadence of a god. This man was laughably average. Slabs of fear began to crumble and fall away from James' chest. Maybe there was a simple misunderstanding. Maybe there was a rational explanation.

"Dr. Grant?" James asked.

The man nodded and lowered his hand, realizing that James had still not shaken it.

"Yes. What can I do for you?" he asked, his voice a smoothly swirling oil slick in James' ear. No expression had yet crossed his face. He didn't seem to blink, either.

"I'm . . . I'm missing my daughter. She's supposed to be here, right here," James lifted the empty blanket higher so the doctor could see, "but she's not. Everyone else seems to think she is, though. Everyone else sees her. But I don't. There's nothing here."

The doctor motioned to a wall from which jutted a thing that resembled the offspring of a pyramid and a honeycomb.

"What do you see there?" he asked.

James shrugged.

"A weird shape."

"Nothing more?" the doctor asked.

James shook his head no.

The doctor pointed at another figure rising out of the floor—an inverted trapezoidal-starlike configuration.

"And there?"

"Pretty much the same. What does this have to do with my daughter?"

James' extremities were beginning to ache from the room's temperature.

"Don't you see the beauty? What are these things? What are these shapes? Impossibilities. They are nothing. They are created, but they are ultimately nothing. You could no more describe this place than you could the idea of zero or infinity. And we are all children here. You, your wife, myself. Your daughter."

James was losing his patience quickly. He was freezing to death while the doctor provided nothing but quasi-mystical babble.

"I don't understand. Where is my daughter? Where is she?"

The doctor pointed at the blanket then spread his hands wide, in a gesture of expansiveness.

"Right there. Nowhere. Everywhere," he said. "Let me show you something that will help clear up this matter entirely."

The doctor raised his hand to his own face and dug his nails into the flesh of his cheek. James watched, dumbstruck and disturbingly fascinated. His stomach flipped end over end.

As the doctor pressed harder and his fingers sank into the fatty tissues, blood began to flow down his jawline and drip onto his coat. At no time did he wince or make even the slightest sound. He simply plunged his fingers deeper within his face, into layers of muscle and bone. Balling up his hand and yanking backward quickly, the doctor suddenly tore one side of his face away. From eye socket to mouth, only wet, glistening skull was left.

James doubled over and vomited. When he glanced up between heaves, he realized that the doctor wasn't finished.

"What the hell?" James muttered. "What the hell?"

The doctor was tearing the rest of his face off with one hand while the other was battering his skull with already ragged knuckles.

As James clamored for air, he heard a series of cracks.

"No, no, no, no," he stammered. He lifted his gaze and lost all sense of reality. There, standing no more than four feet away, was the doctor, fully erect, arms crossed, with a deep, placid, penetrating blackness in place of his upper head. It was stark absence. The doctor moved toward James and his tongue dropped away, hitting the floor with a heavy splosh. Only his lower jaw, still covered in skin and beard, remained above his neck as a human reminder.

James straightened and backed away. This could not be real. This had to be a psychotic episode.

"You see now?" the doctor's voice undulated through the air, "You see the truth? What are you?"

The doctor reached out to touch James' shoulder, but James managed to slink backward, closer to the door.

"What are you?"

James turned and bolted for the exit but it was, as he already subconsciously knew, a false hope. He tried the knob, but it was locked from the outside.

The doctor, the thing—whatever he or it was—casually strode up behind James. He could feel the pulsing chill of it on his back. The doctor leaned in and spoke to James' neck. It was too close. It was too dense, too massive. James' sinuses started to throb. His sense of balance was also fading.

"What are you?" the doctor asked again.

James twisted around and met the abyss. The darkness enveloped him, probing his nostrils and mouth. The pressure behind his eyes was building ever greater. This couldn't be real. It simply couldn't. It made no sense.

"What are you?"

The darkness pounded inside James' being.

"What are you?" James screamed.

"What are you?" The question more insistent, heavier than before.

"James Dodd," he answered through the intense pain rising in his head. He felt disconnected, as if he might pass out.

"What are you?" The doctor's voice reached into James' brain and squeezed. A thin trickle of blood ran out his nose.

"An accountant! A father!" James cried out. "Human! What do you want me to say?"

"What are you? What were your parents? What is your daughter? What will her daughter be? What are you? What are they? What is the nature of everything and everyone that ever has been or ever will be?"

The emptiness crushed James' life under the weight of its insistence. He felt something burst in the back of his head, a searing coldness. In one fractional instant, he understood.

"Nothing," he answered, and fell to the floor in a heap of ruptured belief.

Twenty minutes later, James, tightly gripping the empty blanket to his chest, wandered back into Dawn's room. His stride was less hesitant, less haphazard than when he had left. He moved forward in a straight line to Dawn. His eyes were frozen forward, unblinking and unrolling, as if encased in the head of a wax figurine.

"Where have you been?" Dawn asked. Both anger and relief snaked around her question.

James didn't respond. He simply rocked the balled up blanket in his arms and laughed—an echoing, cracked sound without blood or sunshine coursing beneath its pitch.

"James, where have you been?" Dawn asked again, impatience creeping in. "What were you doing with Samantha?"

"She's so beautiful," he answered. "I was out with my little girl. We went for a walk."

The reply was not a defense for his absence or an incitement to verbal combat; it was a statement of fact: pure, simple, and even. Any subtext had been purged from James' voice.

"Where did you go?"

James stared at Dawn, his mouth slack.

He couldn't remember.

Only vague outlines of images floated through his head. The events surrounding his visit to Dr. Grant were little more than an unconnected series of dots that took no recognizable shape.

"Just . . . out. I talked to the nurse. I walked around for

a while. I don't know. It doesn't matter. I'm here now and I'm fine and Samantha's here and she's perfect and healthy and . . . look . . . isn't she beautiful, hon? Look at that chin! It's exactly like your mom's."

He swiveled the swaddled bundle toward Dawn and crouched so that it was level with her vision, then carefully slid it into her arms. Concentrated joy washed over Dawn's face. She fingered the blanket edges back to reveal more emptiness.

"It is like mom's," she said, tears welling up in her words.

"My princess," James murmured. "My world."

"What do you think she'll be when she's grown? What will she be like?" Dawn asked quietly, stroking space.

"Everything," James replied, beaming. "Anything."

The couple sat in quiet contemplation.

A woman in a room nearby screamed, cracking the pristine silence. Neither James nor Dawn looked up.

After a few more minutes passed, James began to softly sing a lullaby to the nothingness. Dawn smiled. James couldn't wait to take his daughter home.

Critical Theory

She closed the book, placed it on the table, and, finally, decided to walk through the door. Though her back now slouched, her knees now cracked, and her hands trembled with the palsy of anxious decades, she felt, if for only a precious moment, as though she were that hopeful seven-year-old girl who had been brought here by the men in red suits so long ago.

When they'd come, her parents had cried and her older brother had screamed "Monsters!" over and over again. But she hadn't seen monsters; she'd only seen very normal men in strange, shiny crimson suits. They made her father sign papers—which he did with shaking hand— then carried her to a gleaming white van and fed her a tiny pink candy that caused her to fall asleep. She awoke in the white-walled room, the only room she'd know for eternities, with a book and a table and a bed and a chair. One of the men in the red suits stood inside the room with her; in a ghostly, hollow voice, he told her that she must stay in the room and read the book until instructed otherwise. He said that if she tried to leave through the door—a door that, he claimed, would always remain standing open—her parents and her brother would all die painful, gruesome deaths. He said her brother would be burned alive inside a car and her father would commit suicide by drinking bleach and her mother would be crushed beneath the wheels of a bus. He said that the only way to prevent these terrors, these horrors, was to remain in the room and read the book; if the girl could figure out what the book meant, he said, then maybe, just maybe, she could leave the room and her family could live.

So, the girl had stayed. And the girl had read.

The book was long—thousands of pages long—and written in a language the girl understood but that seemed to be used in some ephemeral, ambiguous way. Words she knew didn't mean what they normally meant and phrases she had heard her parents use were used in entirely different contexts. Her mind ached every day, every night; she tried to glean meaning from the pages, tried to save her loved ones, but understanding was slow in coming.

And all the while, she grew. She became a woman in silence, in thought.

Years passed and still the men in the red suits continued to bring her food and water whenever she spoke to the walls and asked for them; they continued to tend to her excretory needs and her grooming. And, each day, one of them would ask her if she understood the book yet, and she would hazard half-guesses and grasping interpretations to which the men would simply reply "Keep going."

And so, thinking always of her family, always of their safety, always of their forevers, on she read and on she puzzled with only the encouragement of "Keep going," until finally, one day, no one came when she asked for sustenance. As she grew parched and starved, she cried out and screamed at the walls, but the men in the red suits did not come. The woman continued reading, continued unraveling mysteries, but rescue did not arrive.

Dying, she knew, fate against fates, that she must walk through the door. She stood on its threshold, nervous, excited, terrified, sorrowful, guilty, and joyous.

"It means . . ." she whispered, "it means everything."

And she stepped through.

Four is Enough

I have no more unessential parts to sell. I type with one hand. I read with one eye. I speak with half a tongue. I no longer have legs to walk upon. My abdomen has been carved time and again, muscle and fat shorn like bacon. I really can't spare my remaining lung, but who knows? That might have to go, too, eventually. There is almost nothing left for anyone to eat. And yet the tuition bills pile ever higher and the rent is paid ever later.

That's why, today, I'm here to sell a finger. Just one. Four is still enough. With four, I can still model universes and mash keyboards. I can probably even handle the electron collider controls. It won't be so bad. I've certainly had worse extractions. Besides, that one finger should provide the means to live another month. I have to give it up. Only one more. I can make due with four.

Sitting here, in the repository waiting room, is always the worst part of the process. You have three options while you're here. One, you can stare at the other supps. Two, if you're a suppi-vore, you can go into the storefront and browse the newest products. Give a little, take a little, I guess. Three, you can stare at the slip of paper they give you—your listing. Mine reads:

Base modifier—COGNITIVE, subheading KNOWLEDGE /INTELLECT, subheading PHYSICS, subheading SCIENCE, subheading STUDENT

$3,500/oz.

Cut—finger (pinky)

Individual—university student in theoretical physics, male, aged 22, multiple academic awards

Mental illnesses—none known

Genetic diseases—none known

Threat of prion contamination—very low

Benefits—increased analytical capability and perception, potential expansion of physics, astronomy, and mathematics knowledge

Side effects—potentially lowered self esteem, lethargy, indecisiveness, development of interested in classical philosophy, development of interest in science-fiction literature and movies, development of interest in robotics /artificial intelligence

Grade—B+

This is a normal listing for me. It'll eventually end up affixed to a little shrink-wrapped package with morsels of myself inside.

Most vores will only purchase supplements if they're Grade C or better. Below C, you might as well not even try to sell. No profit. I've heard of supps losing entire organs for less than one hundred dollars. I'm lucky to be graded B+. I get a decent return.

A friend once told me that, back when biologists first discovered that information was stored in subatomic particles and could be passed on through physical ingestion, anyone graded below A-level wasn't even allowed to sell. Now, thrifty vores and info addicts can easily pick up cheap F-level and D-level supplements at discount repositories. They get what they pay for. Sometimes their brains disintegrate. Tarsen's Disease. Sometimes their organs erupt in spontaneous bleeding. MORS. Multiple Organ Rejection Syndrome. Sometimes they even end up less mentally or physically gifted than before. It's possible. Rare, but possible.

I quickly grow bored with reading my listing. I can only scan the same words so many times before they lose all meaning. So I watch the other supps.

Across the room I see a woman who's almost entirely gone. A blind stump. No nose or ears, either. Her listing is taped to her chest. I wonder how she gets here. Maybe she's indebted to a vore who carries her in. Creditors sometimes do that if they're particularly generous.

The hammer of a muted bell thuds off the walls and falls flat to the floor. Next supp.

"Pollard. Pollard, frontal lobe, second deposit."

A bald man with recent cranial supplication staggers to his feet. His mouth practically hangs off his face. His eyes are muddy. The nurse leads him away, to the extraction room. I feel nothing for that man. I feel nothing for myself. Sometimes I wonder if emotion doesn't regenerate the way they say it does.

I keep my vision well away from my hand. Never stare at what you're about to deposit. You'll think about how much of you is actually in that piece of yourself. You'll question whether that thing is you or if you are it. You'll start questioning where the "you" of you is located. Your body will either become a devil or a messiah. It's not healthy. Better to look at those things you're certain aren't you. Of course, who can really be sure of what that even is anymore? Right now, dozens of vores, maybe hundreds, are walking the streets with my knowledge spinning inside them, with my fondnesses and hatreds bubbling somewhere under the surface. In a sense, I am them. I look at them and I see myself. I look at myself and I see otherness. Strange ontologies, I suppose.

My point is that you want to avoid what the docs call personal separation anxiety. Psychical fragmentation, essentially.

Another bell thuds.

"Scrimshaw. Scrimshaw, left forearm."

A bedraggled but attractive blonde woman stands. She's missing one arm and one foot but, surprisingly, still retains a pair of large breasts and firm, high buttocks. Since she's a supp, there's no reason to keep those rich mounds of fat and muscle. Antiquated attachments to long-dead ideals of the feminine form don't provide sustenance or shelter. Of course, archaic conceptions of masculine beauty are equally meaningless; gonad supplication funded my third semester, bicep supplication paid for last year's rail pass, and pectoral supplication is still helping keep me in electricity for eight hours every day.

Someone clears his or her throat. There's a shuffling of papers and a shuffling of feet.

My mind wanders to my project.

I'm in my last year of study. My thesis: The Manifestation of Dark Matter as Zero-Point Energy and Quantum Constant. I've got it all mapped. The force that propels the expansion of the universe is the same that holds matter together at a quantum level. It's unobservable, but it's reality. A dualistic force that simultaneously tears apart macrocosmically and compresses microcosmically. I have the equations to prove it. My idea is going to win the Nobel Prize. Youngest recipient in its long history. I'm sure of it. If only I can finish. But first I have to deal with my tuition. Two hundred and sixty thousand dollars this year. A deficit that's led me to the dusky downtown repository yet again.

A woman sits down next to me. About my age. Brunette. One leg. Both arms, but missing several fingers. Might have had some muscle layers stripped from the remaining leg. It seems shrunken. One crackling green eye.

She notices me watching.

"Hi," she says.

"Hi," I murmur. It's difficult to enunciate with a halved tongue.

The clock sheds minutes.

I hear a moan. It could be from a man or a woman. Its pitch resides in a pleasant middle ground.

The woman beside me turns and stares at me.

"How many does this make for you?" she asks.

"Nineteen," I say.

She nods.

"This is only my seventh."

A pause.

"Do you ever wish you were at the end? At the stage of completion?" she asks.

"No," I say, not even thinking. "I plan to stop before I hit it. I'm in college. Almost finished, too. I'll have a career-track job soon. I'll be able to stop then."

She nods.

"I went to college for a year," she says. "That was when I did my first and second supplications. I didn't finish. College, that is. I dropped out and devoted myself to my writing. Foolish, maybe. Probably."

"You're a writer?" I ask.

"Yeah."

Someone stifles a cough.

"Crimson blades crushed underfoot,

occluded by a spire's shade,

do dance and wave

in future time

sent to an early grave."

I have no idea what she said. The words make sense individually. Together, I'm not so sure. I don't ask the meaning.

"You're a . . . poet?"

"I try," she says. "But I've never sold any of my poems. No one wants them. So I give them away. That one's yours now."

I'm unsure what to say.

"Thank you. It was . . . um . . . pretty."

An eyebrow shoots up, its point condemning my assessment.

"Pretty?" she asks. "That wasn't what I was going for, but okay."

I hate aesthetics. I don't know how to wrap myself around them. They're so organic, so unquantifiable.

"Sorry. I'm terrible with words. I study physics. Theoretical physics. If that makes you feel any better."

She smiles, one side of her mouth raised higher than the other. Feline, perhaps.

"It's okay. Poetry isn't for everyone. Some vore is probably out there using my supplements to write love sonnets to a girlfriend or boyfriend who doesn't understand them, either. But at least someone's listening. You listened, too. That's all I can ask. Besides, I suck at math, so you're ahead of me in that physics game."

I shrug.

"Everyone's good at something," I say. "If we weren't, we couldn't give."

"Trucr words, my friend. Truer words."

I think that's an ancient colloquialism. I'm not sure. I'm not sure of much outside my own work anymore.

A man is wheeled out of the extraction room. Full facial supplication. No eyes, no ears, no lips or nose, and most of his cheeks hollowed. I think he's grinning.

The poetess points at the stump of a woman across the room.

"Do you think she's here for her completion?"

I shake my head.

"No. Not yet. Not without someone accompanying her. A creditor or her next of kin. Someone to collect the final payment. Completionists always have someone with them."

The poetess nods.

"So what are you giving today?" she asks.

"Finger. Just one. Last one."

"Really? That's what I'm giving, too. It'll leave me with seven, and I don't use my right hand to write, anyway, so I have at least two more to spare before I need to make any tough decisions."

Tough decisions. I've never thought about supplication as a tough decision. It's just the means to an end.

It's how you pay the bills. Supps give, vores eat or inject, and the world turns. There's no point in torturing yourself over it. I don't understand some people.

"Have you ever thought about just . . . running away from it all?" the poetess asks.

"I can't really run anywhere," I say.

She bursts into laughter, which I don't understand, either. Some of the supps jump or shake at the disruption of stillness.

"What? I can't. Really. Look at me."

I pat the nubs of former legs.

Her laughter dies somewhere deeper than her throat. She stares at me.

This woman disturbs me. I just want to give my supplement and leave.

"Nevermind," she says.

I can't imagine what's taking so long. Usually the wait isn't this bad.

"Do you ever wonder if some of the vores think they're gods?" the poetess asks.

I shake my head. Crazy question. A poet's question, obviously.

"No."

"Really? Even though they're getting smarter and faster and stronger and more able to do everything? I mean, what are we doing here but offering up sacrifices? We're god enablers. We're worshiping what doesn't even exist yet. Our faith is a system of slow destruction, and only the vores will end up in heaven."

"I could never worship the vores. They're just people," I say. "I'd hate them before I worshiped them."

Her eye narrows to a sliver.

"You can hate your god, you know," she says.

I wave off her comment with my full, unextracted hand.

"This is just a means to an end, a financial transaction, not a religion."

A moment of uneasy deliberation creeps in between us.

"And you really don't wish you could be at the stage of completion?" she asks. "Really?"

She's tried this line of inquiry already.

"No," I say again.

"You're too much like the rest, then," she whispers, not really to me at all. "Sad."

Silence sweeps over the room.

Sometimes I wish I could hide forever inside my apartment and work on my project. I'm so close. So close. No people, no distractions. No parsing broken conversations for hidden meanings and halved interpretations. No. None of that. Only me and my ideas. Me and my equations. Me and my computer models. All logical and calculable. Knowable. So much simpler.

The bell thuds.

"Gearhardt. Gearhardt, digit, right hand."

That's me.

"That's me," I say.

The poetess gouges me with a cyclopean needle.

"Go on then," she says.

I nod and slide into my powerchair. It's always linked to my particular brainwave patterns. I think *toward the nurse* and the chair moves off in the direction of the nurse, who's standing by the door to the prep rooms, holding a clipboard with all my pertinent health and financial information.

I look back.

The poetess is watching me, her mouth held in a purse of what might be disappointment or what might be anger. It's too hard to tell which is more likely. I don't have time to weight the options and, in all honesty, I don't really care.

The nurse holds the door open for me and I buzz through. She follows.

"Room 5, Mr. Gearhardt," she says from a place over my head.

I roll along until I reach Room 5.

The nurse opens the door to the small waiting space and holds out one hand.

"Your listing, please."

I place the paper in her palm and accidentally brush her fingers. They're icy and rough. I don't like that I've touched them. Tactile loathing.

"Please wait in the room for the next available technician."

I roll past her, into the room. The door snaps shut.

I wait. Again.

I survey the room's décor: stainless steel examination table, stainless steel skin, stainless steel cabinet upon which rests a row of empty test tubes, and a poster that lists the current exchange rates for various grades and supplement types. It's an unsettled space, a space that could change in use or form at any moment because it's so empty.

A technician knocks on the door and enters before I even have time to consider whether I should answer. Not that I would want to prevent him from entering, anyway.

"Mr. Gearhardt?" he says, reading off the tablet he's

carrying.

"Yes," I answer.

"You're here for a digit extraction, correct?"

"Yes."

"And you've already had extensive extraction done before?"

"Yes."

"Good. Good. Have you ever taken supplements, yourself? Are you a known carrier of any genetic diseases or suffer from any serious psychological infirmities?"

"No. None of those."

His eye remains glued to the tablet. My eye remains glued to his tablet. I wonder what secrets they've disencoded from my DNA. It's all right there on the screen, but only technicians can read a supplicant's personal information. He could be divining my destiny for all I know.

"Excellent," the technician says. "Then you're ready for extraction. You are aware of the current exchange rate for your grade and base modification qualities?"

"Yes."

"Good. Any questions, Mr. Gearhardt?"

"No. I've done it before. This is minor."

"That it is, Mr. Gearhardt. Please follow me."

Time to go. The technician leads me through overly lit hallways. The extraction room isn't far ahead.

Before we even reach it, I hear the surgical laser inside, humming a monotone concerto to itself. If it wasn't so unerring, someone might call it beautiful. But not me.

I roll past the blinding halogen of the halls and enter the room. A bank of anesthetics and syringes glitters to my left. The laser glows to my right; the technician strolls to its control panel.

"Please move in front of the L.E.T.," the technician says.

Light Extraction Tool, he means. I roll up to its cool, calming snout.

"Okay. Let me give you a shot of chloroprocaine and we'll begin."

The technician moves to the bank of anesthetics and rifles through some syringes. I simply stare at the tip of the laser.

This will be the last. One more phalange for the rest of my life. Yes, this will definitely be the last. My work is too important. It has to be completed. I have a future beyond this room and a vore's stomach. I know it. I will not reach the stage of completion. Yes, I still have debt. I will always have debt. But this has to be the last. This *will* be the last. I have faith.

Take All Your Troubles

The first time she died, she was five years old. A television commercial—one of those "Save the Starving Children" misery collages—rang clear and true with her budding sense of empathy. There, on the screen, she saw a boy of roughly her age squatting in a mud hole, flies swarming his eyes and mouth. As he breathed, his ribs drew taut against his skin, threatening to tear free from his body and the agony it had been ordained to endure.

She asked her mother "Why does that boy look like that but I don't?" and her mother, more focused on a household chore than the suffering of a world that had always suffered, answered quietly "Because he's starving and you're not."

She locked eyes with the boy and, sensing a kinship with him, searched him out, though she didn't know how. Her mind roamed over the earth until she found him lying in the shadow of the reaper's ebon wings in an arid mission hospital. She felt the hollow spaces, the fear, the certainty of nothingness that resided inside him, and she pulled it all away, into herself. The hunger, the fever, the hopeless tomorrows, she took it all and crushed it up into a ball and buried it within her stomach or somewhere deeper. She felt hot, hotter than she ever had, and cold, colder than any day she'd spent in the snow without mittens or a jacket. She felt something like loneliness and something like falling, something like anger and something like flying.

And then, in a way, she died.

When she came to, in a hospital days later, her parents talked in circles around a "mystery condition" that mimicked severe starvation and dehydration. They didn't know, couldn't know, that on the opposite side of the planet an emaciated boy had, suddenly and without reason, leaped from his deathbed and run laughing through his village, miraculously nourished and vital for the first time in his life. They couldn't know that their daughter had taken his death and stored it away in herself, had experienced his dying and his piteous end so that he wouldn't have to. They only knew that their daughter was sick and they only knew what medicine could explain.

But the girl knew differently. She realized what she'd done and she understood the gift she had been granted. She held the power to strip death off its victims provided that she wore a weakened version of that very same death herself. She could save anyone. She could save everyone. As long as she was willing to suffer.

And so she began her great project, what she would later call "The Amelioration." At first, she thought of herself as a saint in miniature, volunteering in nursing homes, tearing away infirmities from the elderly so that they might have a few more years of creaking conscious-ness. As she aged and grew, she candy-striped in cancer wards and ICUs, she spent weekends at drug addiction clinics and soup kitchens, and all the while she died and died again, hoarding death upon death that was not her own.

She began to imagine herself not as a saint but as a martyr, a messiah. So often was she rushed to doctors' offices and emergency rooms, pulse nearing flatline; so many textures of destruction did she feel, so many contours of death's hand. And while she became ever more familiar with the wide variety of pain that formed the foundation of the universe, she became a woman.

Years passed, and the woman kept herself close to decay so that she could, at least for a time, arrest its in-exorable progress. She found work as a nurse and, in the role of haloed Nightingale, imbibed of diseases mundane and exotic. She licked cancer's sour, black tentacles and hugged the crushing tread of heart failure to her chest; she spun wildly in the throes of Parkinson's and drifted into Alzheimer's impenetrable fog. And she endured it all as one who wants nothing more than to cultivate light in dark places.

The woman watched the improbable smiles of loved ones as their dearly almost-departed rushed back from the brink, and those smiles, the gleeful absurdity of those smiles appearing in a time in which happiness should have been banished, were reward enough for her pain.

So she lived and she died for decades, her face hidden behind curtains and in shadows, just out of reach of the miracles she had cast. For sixty years, she nursed, saving those beyond salvation, cheating death of its victories.

Then, one day long after her hands turned venous and her skin wrinkled and sagged, a weight clamped down upon her breast and would not let go. Her breath came up short and an existential fatigue brought her to her knees. In her chest, a heart that had wished nothing on the universe but good will sputtered and failed. The one death she could not prevent had reached her.

As her heart beat its last, the woman's eyes went wide, for there, before her, she saw not a dazzling tunnel or a warm embrace as she had anticipated, but hundreds of thousands of obsidian needles spewing from a fissure within herself. In that moment, she screamed silently and realized that, despite all her effort, she had never destroyed death; rather, she had simply collected it and compressed it inside some unseen space. Miracles are the theft of fate, and fate—that Janus-faced sibling of death—will always have its recompense for what has been stolen. For decades, the woman had tipped a set of scales that had never meant to be tipped. Now, it was finally due to be balanced.

Like an ethereal bomb, the woman burst and the abyssal needles all exploded forth, shooting outward, into the world, into people whose deaths they were never meant to be but, for kindness, they would have to suffer nonetheless.

Bolt

A crack echoes across the underside of the dome. Though it's difficult to pick out in the blaze of white lights, a baseball is screaming through the air somewhere close to the ceiling. Staring toward the beams high above, an imagined audience takes pause and draws in a collective breath that sucks the oxygen from the building and creates a vacuum around this moment, this tiny streaking hope. The occupants of empty seats tense forward, ready to leap to their feet and cheer.

Rapidly, the ball begins to descend, as must all things which reach great heights. It drops with the weight of the world strapped about its circumference and lands, quiet and spent, in an aisle just beneath the giant orange that hangs over the right field seats.

The crowd of no one erupts in raucous, silent cheering. Cowbells clang but do not clang. Airhorns blow but do not blow. Fireworks shoot into the eyes of those who are willing and able to imagine them.

And all the while, standing on home plate, gazing into

a space that only the romantic and the narcissistic can see, is a lanky young man with rugged stubble and purposefully wild, teased-out hair. He pumps his fist once in the air, drops his bat, and begins to trot toward first base. He's wearing a uniform with the name "LONGORIA" stitched across the back, but that's not his name. It was the name of someone else, someone who achieved something of note, something of merit, something that bestowed upon him the right to have random onlookers not just guess at who they might be watching but know, undeniably, incontrovertibly know who was under the shirt. No, "LONGORIA" is not his name. His name is Derrick McCoy, and you've never heard of him.

But you should have.

His face should have graced Wheaties boxes and video game covers. He should have dated starlets and supermodels. His name should have been whispered reverently in the same sentences as Ruth and Williams, Mays and Aaron. You should know who he is. But you never will. His face won't be etched on any gold plaques or marble busts in hallowed halls; it won't adorn thousands of advertisements or be plastered on the walls of any steel coliseums. No one will remember what could have been. They'll only remember what was. And Derrick McCoy almost was. He almost made it into history. Almost. But for the plague.

Six months ago Derrick had no idea what a mitochondrial necrocyte was. He didn't even know the word "revenant" existed. Six months ago, he was just a minor league outfielder with a sweet swing and a quick step. Six months ago, on this very night, he was going three-for-four with two doubles and three runs batted in. It was the same night his manager, a granite-jawed, speech-slurring septuagenarian named Rich Dukes, called him aside in the bottom of the eighth inning and told him to pack his bags. Derrick had just jogged in from right field and was clearing space for himself on the bench when Dukes sidled up beside him and rested a beefy hand on his shoulder.

"McCoy," Dukes spat. The old man seemed to find names—or really any level of address beyond "you" or "kid"—generally unpalatable. "GM in Flor'da called. Rays need ya. Get in the locker room, pack yer crap, an' get down there. They got a plane comin' for ya tonight. Go give 'em hell, kid."

One quick, hesitant pat on the back and the wizened manager turned and hobbled away, yelling something about bunting to the batter in the on-deck circle.

Buried under a sudden avalanche of elation, Derrick stood motionless, breathless, thoughtless. His heart skipped several beats. He was never more alive.

Since he was six years old, he knew he had a gift. He could hit the ball farther and more frequently than anyone else on his tee ball team. He outran most of them, too. He continued outhitting and outrunning all the way through high school. He won golden statuettes and spar- kling crystal trophies. Local sports writers called him a "wunderkind." His coaches called him a "phenom." His teammates simply called him "Bolt," because they said they'd never seen anyone generate as much bat speed. And, indeed, his swing was quick and explosive as lightning; it was the primary factor that led the Tampa Bay Rays to select him in the second round of the amateur draft. Two years later—at only 20—Derrick was mashing at Double A Montgomery and on the fast track to a job as the Rays everyday right fielder. He was on the verge of national recognition, of hacking and slashing his way into the consciousnesses of millions of fans. But, then again, he'd been led to believe that he was on the verge of entering some holy land and accomplishing some other-worldly task ever since he'd pulverized his first tee ball.

By some standards, Derrick had already achieved success. His name had been printed in Sports Illustrated six times in the past three years. He was frequently listed as one of the top twenty prospects in all of baseball. He was already living a life most athletes could only dream about. But it wasn't enough. It wasn't the outer limit of what Derrick knew he could do, what he knew he was supposed to do. The blueprints for greatness were encoded within his DNA, and he intended to follow their instructions.

This call-up to the majors was one of the final steps in building toward that greatness. It was the lower summit of a mountain he had been expected to climb for the past fourteen years. It was his germinal immortality.

Derrick had no vocabulary for the occasion. Had someone asked him how he felt, he could have only answered through smiles and dances, handstands and high-flying jumps. He was reduced to little more than a nebulous haze of pride, elation, and body language. He was so close now. So close to the *je ne sais quoi* that was celebrity.

His feet began to move, and he began to drift toward

the dugout's exit, propelled by either the winds of fate or his own subconscious. It didn't matter which, as long as he was heading in the direction of fame, fortune, and glory.

As he slowly descended the stairs that led to the locker room, a series of firetrucks, ambulances, and police cars blew past the stadium, sirens blaring and lights flashing. It was the fifth time in two hours that such a parade of emergency vehicles had briefly interrupted the game. However, riding high atop his endorphin cloud, Derrick didn't notice this last intrusion. Even if the ground had split asunder and the devil had risen from its flame-spouting fissures, Derrick wouldn't have flinched, so consuming was his self-congratulatory inebriation.

The following hour and a half was entirely missing from his memory, dulled into nonexistence by virtue of being filled with comparative minutiae. At various points he must have changed into street clothes, driven to his hotel room, packed a suitcase, called his family, and driven to the airport because, at midnight, he found himself reclining comfortably in a densely cushioned seat aboard a privately chartered flight from Montgomery to St. Petersburg. Across the aisle, a squat middle-aged man in a bulging Tampa Bay Rays polo shirt and khaki pants flipped through a packet of papers, many of which displayed little more than columns and rows of numbers.

The man glanced at Derrick.

"So, from what I can tell, you'll probably make the lineup in two days. Tomorrow night I think we'll just keep you on the bench and give you some time to adjust, to get used to the atmosphere and let the thrill settle a bit. Then the next night, you'll get a start in right. Sound good?"

Derrick nodded.

This portly man—probably an assistant something-or-other to someone with administrative power—clearly held the keys to the mansion in which Derrick had been yearning to reside his entire life. He could hear promise jingling in the man's pockets.

Minutes passed in relative silence. The man in the polo shirt continued riffling through his papers.

"What do you think about these riots?" he asked, never glancing up. "Crazy stuff, huh? Hope we don't have to cancel any games because of them."

"Riots?" Derrick asked, shifting in seat, concerned about anything that might impact his debut or his playing time.

"Yeah. Riots. That's what the news is calling them. Started this morning, apparently. They're everywhere. Across the U.S., in Canada, Mexico, and a couple in Europe, too. In St. Petersburg, there were six or seven of them reported before I left to meet you."

"What are people rioting about? Something political?"

The man dropped the sheets of statistics onto his lap and met Derrick's eyes.

"Well, that's the question," he said. "It's weird, because, from what I understand, people aren't really rioting. They're sort of grouping together and attacking other people—bystanders, police, old women, little kids, anybody. The news said a couple people were killed and a bunch were injured. And, like I said, this is happening everywhere. Scary stuff."

"Terrorism?" Derrick offered, hiding behind the comfort of the zeitgeist.

The stout man shrugged.

"Who knows? If it's terrorism, it's the most well-organized, most widespread, and most random act of terrorism ever conceived. But, I'm sure it will all be under control when we get back. It's just crazy shit."

Derrick slouched back in his seat, needles in his stomach. Riots were not good. Riots meant fear, fear meant self-imposed isolation, and self-imposed isolation meant low attendance at baseball games. Derrick could only hope that the riots—or whatever they were—didn't interfere with attendance. Without the fans, the game had no meaning, no resonance beyond the perimeter of the diamond. All the home runs or stolen bases in the world were meaningless unless people—as many people as possible—witnessed their spectacle and assigned to them some sort of significance. Without the fans, Derrick was as good as mired in anonymity's crowded, shit-washed gutter.

He turned to the window and stared out into a dark void of undifferentiated, unlit, uncaring sky, land, and sea; it was everything that the searingly angelic brightness of a stadium in its full electrified finery was not.

Derrick stands along the first base line, signing a baseball for an expectant fan, a spectral boy of nine or ten. He scribbles "To Jonathan—Keep swinging for the moon! Derrick McCoy" then flips the ball at a vacant blue seat in the first row. It bounces off the seat's hard plastic back and disappears behind the wall that separates the field from the stands, the player from the spectator, the remembered from the forgotten. Derrick can't see the ball's final resting spot, but he's sure it's in the hands of a deserving young admirer. He turns and trots into the dugout, ready to snatch up his helmet and bat and step to the plate once again. The missing crowd is rocking the dome apart tonight, and rightfully so. Derrick had already sent three pitches deep and the Rays are leading nine to four.

A long-dead announcer calls out "Right fielder, number two, Derrick McCoy!" The silence of his name rings from the P.A. system.

Beaming, Derrick pulls on his batting gloves and strides toward the last stage on earth.

Behind the first base wall, the ball Derrick just signed rests amongst a vast pile of other baseballs, both new and old, crisp white and dusty eggshell. All of them are variously inscribed with first names and motivational phrases and the jagged signature "Derrick McCoy." All of them are cherished treasures dedicated to nobody.

Derrick couldn't sleep, not with only a weak lock and chain separating himself from the gunshot pops and distant screams that occasionally scratched at the walls of his hotel room. Sirens spread their screeching wings in his brain; what seemed like blue and red fireworks flashed against the drawn curtains. The world was falling apart. He was supposed to be a star in ascendancy to the heavens, a freshly minted idol for the city, but here, on this night, he felt no brighter or more awe-inspiring than a thirty-watt bulb in the lamp of a funeral parlor. For the first time in his life, he was frightened of something other than failure.

On the ride from the airport to the hotel, Derrick and his stoic driver—a slight Latino man who didn't utter a syllable or peel his vision from the road for even a second—had passed crashed cars, burning houses, police barricades, and impromptu militias standing on street corners, rifles and handguns at the ready. At one stoplight, a bloodied homeless man approached the car and repeatedly smashed his face against the passenger's side window, gnashing his teeth as if he was trying to chew his way through the glass. At another light, two middle-aged women in tattered evening dresses crouched over a third woman lying prone and unmoving at the edge of the crosswalk; Derrick couldn't tell whether they were trying to resuscitate a downed friend with CPR or pounding on a stranger's chest in blind fury.

Clearly, the riot situation had not yet been resolved.

Derrick lay propped up in bed, watching TV with the sound muted. Every station was carrying live coverage of what newscasters could only refer to as "mass panic" and "widespread violence." In New York, Times Square was littered with corpses, gastric fruits erupting from the blossoms of their torn abdomens; in Boston, Fenway Park was ablaze, the Green Monster a crackling wall of Dis; in Washington, D.C., the polished steps of the Capitol Building were streaked with dark tones of crimson; and in St. Petersburg—which didn't even make the national news roundup—Derrick had only to stumble to the window and stare six flights downward, to the sidewalk below, to see a man feverishly clawing at the face of another man who was very much unconscious and, potentially, already dead.

Derrick didn't know much about civil disobedience, but this omnivorous barbarity—the face-ripping, entrailexposing, landmark-burning and all—seemed to him an extreme and unlikely manifestation of political or social upheaval. The back of his head tingled with the sense that something wasn't right in a way he could never begin to articulate. He sunk lower into the bed and contemplated calling his parents or one of his friends.

What if this night doesn't end? he wondered. What happens if civilization crumbles? What do I do? Who wants a hero like a pro athlete or a movie star when you and the people around you become the heroes of your own lives?

On some base, unconscious level, Derrick understood he had no cache in a post-apocalyptic hellscape. Though he couldn't articulate the sentiment in words, he realized that in all the movies about the end of the world, the only heroes are the people who save other people or stop the world from ending. There is no such thing as fame in those movies. There is no glory. Just survival. The survivors are the heroes, but no one's left to call them that.

As he was twisting his mind in tight knots over these issues, the phone rang.

He sat up and glanced at the clock. It was 3:39 AM. Any call made at 3:39 in the morning was bound to be drenched in tears or alcohol. In either case, it probably wouldn't help relieve his anxiety.

Derrick picked up the receiver and cleared his throat.

"Hello?" he answered.

"Hello," a starchy female voice responded. "Is this Derrick McCoy?"

"Yeah, that's me."

"Mr. McCoy, I'm calling on behalf of the Tampa Bay Rays organization. As part of our excellent group of players and staff, you need to be notified of the following announcement by the commissioner of Major League Baseball, sent out to all affiliated teams early this morning. The statement reads: 'In light of the recent violence in many major metropolitan areas, the risk of holding major sporting events has been deemed too dangerous. Any injury or loss of life to spectators, players, crew, or staff would be entirely unacceptable. Therefore, in order to negate any potential harm to all those involved with Major League Baseball and its operations, all regular season games will be suspended until further notice.' "

Derrick's chest collapsed. He felt shorter somehow, a man with a retractable spine and a telescopic soul.

"Now, I've been given a memo saying that you were just called up to the team . . . ah . . . hmmm . . . last night? Is that correct?" the woman asked.

Derrick mumbled something he thought sounded like "yes." The woman on the phone must have thought so, too, because she continued almost without pause.

"Okay then. You don't have to report to the stadium until someone from the team calls you again. We'll let you know when we're going to hold a practice. In the meantime, your hotel and any room services you order will be fully comped. Any questions, Mr. McCoy?"

There were dozens of questions to be asked. Was he supposed to remain sequestered in a hotel room indefinitely? Was there any way he could fly home until games resumed? Was he still guaranteed a roster spot when the season restarted? The only question that spurted from Derrick's mouth, however, was "Why are you calling me at almost four in the morning to tell me this?"

"Because some members of the grounds crew and

stadium security were due to report for work at five o'clock," the woman replied. "The executive decision was made to inform all staff, crew, and players at once, before anyone left the safety of their homes. If you have any further questions, you can call . . ."

The name and number of the person Derrick might have been able to contact for support were cut off by his setting the phone receiver back in its cradle. He didn't want to hear any more. He didn't want to talk any more, either. He was so close to the prize, so close to playing in front of tens of thousands of fans and hearing their tremendous roar, the sound of humanity rising to rage against the prison of its own mediocrity, that he could smell the tang of mustard-drenched hot dogs, taste the dry savoriness of infield dust, and feel the vibration of applause against his skin. He was so close he didn't want to breathe again, for fear of setting in motion a chain of events that might rob him of, quite literally, major league opportunity.

He stumbled from the bed to the window and looked outside. From his eighth story room, he imagined he could almost see the top of the Trop's dome. It was just over the horizon, just beyond the rise of the next gently sloped hill. So tantalizingly close. But so tantalizingly close was where it might lie forever.

Derrick crept back to bed, threw the sheets over his head, and waited for exhaustion to sweep him closer to his dreams.

Crouching several feet off second base, calves tensed, Derrick has nothing to lose. His team is up by seven, there are no outs, and it's a one-and-one count on the batter. He might as well try to take third. The pitcher on the mound, a tall, spider-like figment, never even checks to see how much of a lead Derrick's taken to the base. As the pitcher lowers his hands and begins to draw back his arm in an exaggerated windup, Derrick pounces. Terrified of his speed and his desire, the ground beneath his feet flees from his path. He is wind in a jar, fire on the ocean floor.

By the time the pitcher's lazy curveball finally snaps into the catcher's glove in Derrick's mind, he's already sliding, head-first, into third base; there's no possibility of a throw down the line.

Derrick stands and nods to the invisible crowd. A weak stream of obligatory handclapping trickles down to the field. The fans never get pumped by stolen bases. It doesn't matter. Hits, long balls: those are for the fans. Steals are for the team, for his brothers-at-arms. As if on cue, twelve disembodied smiles appear, Cheshire cat-like, from the shadowed dugout. The batter—Derrick can't decide if he's a burly, pull-hitting, strikeout-prone first baseman or a wiry, spray-hitting, speed demon of a center fielder—rests his bat against his thigh and points both incorporeal index fingers at Derrick, signaling his respect. With a casual, practiced dignity, Derrick points back and laughs.

This is true camaraderie. This is true friendship. This is what being part of a team is all about.

Back in the dugout, a helmet falls from the bench and clatters against the cement floor. Derrick's eyes dart across the diamond. No revenants. Just echoes. Always nothing but echoes.

One day passed. Alone in his hotel room, Derrick watched TV and ordered two meals from room service—both pancakes and eggs. The violence grew more intense, more gruesome, and more bizarre. Reporters claimed that rioters, apparently losing their higher mental faculties, had begun to exhibit primitive cannibalistic behavior. In most major metro areas, death tolls were already speculated as reaching into the thousands.

The president addressed the nation in the evening and assured the public that the situation would be controlled, that Army, Marine, and National Guard units were being deployed to the most populous cities in every state and top scientists were investigating the potential causes of the violent eruptions.

Throughout the night, Derrick heard gunshots and sirens, shouting and honking. He did not sleep soundly.

Two days passed. Derrick, glued to the TV, ordered only one meal from room service. News stations were beginning to talk about the "impossible reanimation of the dead," things called "revenants," and some sort of parasitic microbe that made its home in the energy producing part of cells—a "mitochondrial necrocyte," pathologists termed it.

During the day, he saw two patrols of camouflaged men with automatic rifles and flame throwers stroll past the hotel. One of them gunned down a man limping across the street. The other immolated the body and heaved it, still smoldering, into a black bag, which they dragged onto the sidewalk.

Derrick spent most of the nighttime hours in the unstaffed hotel bar, stealing shots of bourbon and scotch and mournfully singing "Take Me Out to the Ballgame."

Three days passed. A horde of revenants—at least fifteen or twenty in total—broke into the hotel lobby, killed the four security guards who had been standing watch by the front doors, and devoured most of the remaining hotel staff. Derrick learned of the attack from a trembling, stuttering maid he found crouched in the elevator. He offered her some of the liquor that he'd taken from the bar, but she refused any drinks and locked herself in the room across the hall from Derrick's.

Perhaps foolishly or perhaps bravely, Derrick ventured downstairs to aid other survivors. However, he discovered only carnage. The revenants had long since shuffled away, but the remains of their meal were scattered on the tile floor.

An eyeball, torn loose from its owner's socket, stared up from beside Derrick's foot as he stepped out of the elevator and beheld the lobby-cum-abattoir. Piles of rent flesh, shredded organs, and glistening aspic lay in heaps beside what might once have been human bodies. Derrick backed into the elevator and punched the number "8" repeatedly until the brushed silver doors slid shut.

Once he was securely locked in his room again, he ran to the bathroom and dry heaved into the toilet for a half-hour.

During the night he woke several times, sweating and near panic, with visions of bleeding, pulsating, keening landscapes still careening around the inside of his skull.

He was haunted by the lubricious hills of gristle and creaking forests of bone his subconscious had created; both were significantly different settings from his usual nightmares, which tended to involve ejections from World Series Game Sevens and millions of jeering faces.

On the fourth day after his arrival in St. Petersburg, the last of the live television newscasts flipped over to an emergency standby message. Derrick decided to repack his bag and move. No one from the team was going to call him. Baseball was an idle dream that could only be conjured by people who were sleeping soundly—an impossibility now that the world had begun to be shaken from its overlong slumber. The hotel, with its front windows shattered and gaping, was simply no longer safe, either. Revenants could easily storm the building again if they needed snacks. The entire place was a fifteen-story lunchbox waiting to be put to use.

On top of everything else, Derrick was starving. He hadn't eaten anything substantial in two days and, as long as he was sequestered within the hotel, the prospect of finding more than vending machines filled with bags of chips or chocolate bars seemed unlikely.

He had to find new a refuge, a secure, defendable location with ample food sources. His initial thoughts straddled the fence between "grocery store" and "school," but he had no idea where either might be located and it probably wasn't the most intelligent course of action to wander aimlessly in a city teeming with ravenous walking dead and no-nonsense military units operating under martial law. He cursed himself for forgetting his laptop back in Montgomery.

As blind, hurried packing would have it, Derrick was

without the luxury of the internet and its readily supplied maps. He needed to go somewhere that he knew he could reach on foot without getting lost or needing complicated directions—a landmark, maybe, or something he could see from the window of his room. He stared over the low-rising cityscape. The solution was obvious: he had to run to the stadium. Tropicana Field would be his sanctuary, his house of salvation if not his glory. It had few main entrances, hundreds of yards of solid fences, a built-in storehouse of food, and, perhaps most importantly, it was a place of consecration, a place Derrick would be willing to let his corpse rot if he was attacked and killed.

He stowed his clothes and some bathroom accoutrements in his overnight bag and strode to the door. Ten blocks. That's what the portly man on the plane had said. The hotel was ten blocks from the stadium. If Derrick ran fast enough and steady enough, he could survive another week, another month, maybe even a year or more. With time, civilization would surely recover. The game would begin again. And Derrick would be known as the guy who loved his team so much, his sport so dearly, that he weathered the near-apocalyptic storm on the very field upon which he played. He'd be more than "Bolt." He'd be goddamned "Mr. Baseball." He could secure his legend before he even became one. Derrick grinned. Revenants, zombies, whatever. He was beyond it all.

Every entrance is still securely chained and padlocked, every door barricaded and sealed. Once a day, before the game, Derrick monitors the perimeter, a thirty-two ounce Louisville Slugger resting on his shoulder for protection. He's starting to consider leaving the bat inside, since he hasn't even seen a revenant shambling through the parking lot in over three weeks, let alone trying to break into the stadium.

Standing at the main gate, he gazes at the parallel lines of the palm trees that line the walkway to the entrance. A mild autumn wind ruffles their fronds. There is no other movement outside the fence. For a brief, flickering moment, Derrick wonders if he might be the last human being on earth.

What a tremendous honor, he thinks. What an amazing accomplishment. If only someone knew. If only someone could see.

He shrugs and retreats to the inside of the stadium. Once there, he warms a hamburger at one of the food kiosks, eats quickly, then makes his way to the Rays locker room, glancing at his watch. It's 5:02. First pitch is at 7:05 tonight. That means the fans will be arriving soon to watch batting practice. He'd better get out on the field. He wouldn't want to disappoint.

Forty minutes later, after showering and changing into a new uniform—this one has the name "PRICE" stitched across the back—Derrick steps to the plate to take a few practice swings. The pitcher, a squat, barrel-chested, square-shouldered flamethrower, hurls a fastball toward Derrick. He connects with the pitch, but poorly. The ball blasts forward without any elevation. It's headed directly for the pitcher, who does nothing to defend himself. A metallic clang rips through the soft air as the ball hits his torso. The sparse audience gasps. A trainer flies to the mound. Derrick is unimpressed. He's dented this pitcher before. That little guy will be fine. In fact, he winds up and hurls another heater directly over home plate. Derrick clobbers this one. It takes flight, disappearing into the white ceiling of this dead heaven. The fans clap. The fans cheer.

Derrick stares at the scoreboard, all zeros, always all zeros. He knows that someday the power will stop flowing and the scoreboard won't even be lit. Someday he'll be forced to retire. But until that day, he's determined to put on a show for the world. The fans need something to believe in.

Tonight will be another great game.

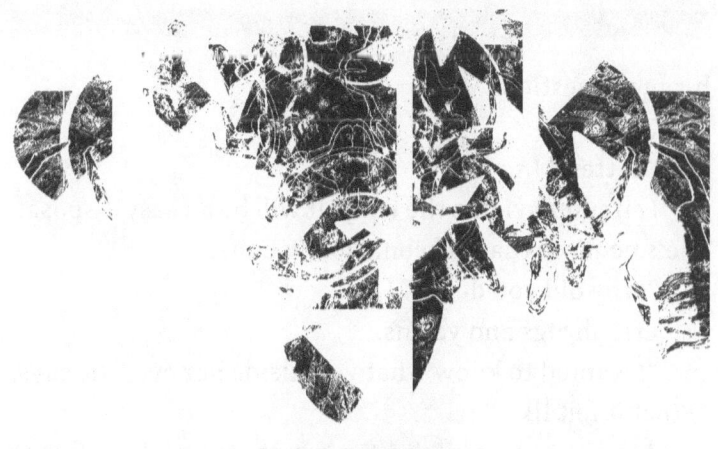

Lessons

Standing over the pale, wispy body, I shake my head. I try to glower and flare my nostrils, but I'm impressed with the precision of the strike. Perhaps even proud. Eric stares at me.

"Did I do wrong?" he asks.

I nudge the body with my foot.

"What have I told you about that word?" I hiss.

Eric sighs.

"It doesn't mean anything," he says, bored with the answer.

"That's right," I say. "So would you like to ask something else?"

Eric stares at me again. His eyes are blue. So blue. Bluer than any sky I've ever gazed into and bluer than any sea I've ever crossed. They're the blue of poets and innocence, the blue of mythical heroes and magic. With those eyes, he could force God himself to lay down his arms. But not me.

"Should I not have done it?" he asks, slowly, unsure of

his own question.

I nod.

"Better," I say.

I circumnavigate the body. It will be an easy disposal. She's no more than fifteen. Mostly bone.

"Why did you do it?" I ask.

Eric shrugs and yawns.

"I wanted to know what was inside her eye," he says. "What it felt like."

Again, I nod. I can't lie. I'm tempted to stick my finger inside the wound, too.

"Well, that's fine," I say. "Daddy has those same questions sometimes. But there's a better time and a better place for this. Now, because you couldn't wait for that time and place, we have a lot of work to do. Are you prepared for that?"

Eric frowns and looks away.

"Well, you'd better be," I say. "We have a long night ahead."

He kicks the floor and mutters something about it all being "unfair."

"Come here," I growl. "And lift the legs as best you can. We'll begin by breaking it all down."

"Come on," Eric whines. "Can't I just go to bed?"

"No," I say. "Now grab a cleaver from the kitchen and help."

I shake my head as he stomps through the house.

Someday I will teach my son how to talk to a girl and how to laugh convincingly, though he feels nothing; someday I will teach my son how to open doors like a gentleman and lock them tightly behind him, so that not even a scream can escape; someday I will teach my son how to tie a gag and sharpen a blade and savor fear in the air.

But tonight I will teach my son only one thing: that burying an icepick in the babysitter's eye is not something he should do unless daddy tells him to.

Forever, in Pieces

February 14th, 1986

Ben cautiously approached the paper bag taped to the side of Monica's desk. Covered in smiley faces and pink blobs that may have been intended as hearts but ended up more closely resembling inverted, misshapen teardrops, the bag hung there, waiting, ready, anticipating more love. It was stuffed full of white, pink, purple, and red envelopes almost to the point of overflow. Something in Ben's stomach turned toward his throat and growled.

He glanced at the desks on either side of Monica's, examining their bags and attempting to feign confusion or indecision. He didn't want to seem too excited about this. Plus, he needed a measure of privacy to do it right. Although she was on the opposite side of the room, ensconced in her own secret deliveries, Ben was still afraid that Monica would spy him dropping the card into her makeshift mailbox. For some reason he couldn't articulate or understand, he needed her to not see his hand slip into the bag. It was better she read the card first. The words were more important than his action.

In one casual motion, Ben dropped his Valentine into the top of the bag and continued walking between desks. He was elated. Even though his palms were sweaty and the thing in his stomach continued to claw softly, the deed was done. Monica would finally know what he couldn't say aloud.

"Okay everyone," Mrs. Flowers yelled above the din of thirty-four scuttling, laughing first-graders. "Finish up and go back to your desks."

Slowly, the room returned to order as everyone took their seats. Ben found his desk, fell into his chair, and realized his palms were freezing.

Mrs. Flowers strode to the front of the room to make another announcement.

"We can take recess now and you can all open your cards during that time. Due to the cold weather, though, we'll be having recess in the gym. You may bring your mailboxes, but remember to pick up all your trash. Now let's go. Single file and calm."

As one, the class ripped their bags from the sides of their desks and ran through the doorway, a galloping herd of anticipation.

Mrs. Flowers sighed and followed.

During recess, Ben sat by himself in a corner of the immense gymnasium. He didn't really have friends, probably because he didn't really talk to anyone; he was never sure what to say and he was always scared that he'd say something stupid that would make everyone hate him. So he talked to himself and played by himself and opened his Valentine's Day mailbox by himself. A typical day, really.

Ben's bag—which he'd decorated with black clouds and yellow lightning bolts—was practically empty. He held it upside-down and four cards spilled out. He tore open the first one, a pink one, in hope that it was from Monica. But no. It was from Jillian. She gave valentines to everyone and didn't even bother to sign them. Her card to Ben featured Strawberry Shortcake boldly proclaiming "You're nice."

Big deal. He threw the card to one side.

The next two he opened were from, respectively, Mrs. Flowers, who scribbled that he was "a wonderful student" on a heart cut from construction paper, and Lucas, who had written the words "Cool dood" on the inside of a G.I. Joe card with a hologram of Snake-Eyes on the front. Lucas was an idiot. All he did was yammer on about how awesome professional wrestling was.

Ben sighed and held up the last card he'd received. It was encased in a gleaming metallic silver envelope that bulged in the middle. Some people stuffed candy hearts or hard candies into their valentines, so he assumed a sweet treat was hidden inside. He carefully slit the top of the envelope with the tip of his fingernail and pulled out the card, an unadorned coal-black rectangle.

He flipped it over.

The back side was the same pitch black surface, only with a few words written on it in what looked like white colored pencil. It read: Ben. We will be together. Wait for me. Forever.

Ben shrugged, having no idea what the note meant,

and shook the envelope over his hand until something dropped out.

And something did drop out: a slender, delicate, pasty white finger. Ben stared at it in disbelief. A finger. He rolled it around in his palm, feeling the softness of its skin against his own. It was well manicured; its nail, painted dark blue and filed to a neat, well-rounded point, protruded several centimeters above the finger's end.

Turning it over, he examined the base, which, while uneven—as if severed hurriedly, perhaps—was almost perfectly smooth. In later years, after he'd researched the possibilities, Ben would attribute this smoothness to a process of surgically precise cauterization. In the moment, though, it didn't matter. Nothing mattered, save the fact that the finger existed and it had been placed in his bag.

He couldn't stop smiling. This was the best Valentine's Day ever. Someone liked him enough to send him something like this, something personal and extraordinary.

He bent the finger, squeezed it, held it in his hand and refused to let go. He didn't understand what it meant or why someone had sent it to him, of all people, but he loved it.

When Mrs. Flowers called recess to an end, he gently placed the card and the finger back in the envelope, folded the entire package in half, and stuck it in his pocket.

Returning to his classroom, Ben saw a crumpled ball lying on the faux-wood top of his desk. He walked to his chair and sat down. Giggles drifted up from somewhere a few aisles away. Something inside Ben, something deeper than his heart or his stomach or all the gooey, bloody parts he couldn't name, collapsed into a spiraling chasm.

He didn't have to pick up the crumpled ball to know what it was. He didn't have to flatten it out and uncrease its edges to know that it was a valentine, that Garfield was on its front, and that a thought bubble containing the words "Let's cuddle" floated above the rotund feline's head. He also didn't have to open it to know that, on the blank interior, he had written the following: "Monica I think I love you. Maybe if you want I could hold your hand in resess. Im not sure if you like me but I hope you do. O.K. Ben."

He wanted to cry. He wanted to run from the room and never face any of these people again, least of all Monica.

But he didn't.

Instead, he rubbed the finger resting cozily in his pocket and tried to imagine Forever.

February 14th, 1989

The snow was falling heavily by mid-morning and the school was abuzz with the expectation that an early dismissal was forthcoming. The Valentine's Day festivities had been crammed into the first two hours of class so that everyone could eat one of Ms. Dunning's homemade brownies and exchange cards before any cancellation went into effect. Homework was even set aside in favor of "quiet socialization time" and computer games.

Normally, Ben would have tried to hop on an Apple IIe to blaze a path across the Oregon Trail, but not today. Despite the snow and the gleeful electricity rebounding off the walls, he had entrenched himself at his desk in the far back corner of the room, alone but for an illustrated edition of The Phantom of the Opera. While his peers devoured chocolate hearts and one another's easy acceptance, Ben alternately read and stared out the window, his mind drifting between the swirling flakes, searching for a reason why his secret love hadn't sent him a greeting today.

After the finger, in two subsequent years, had come a half-dozen teeth and a soft, pale ear, both stuffed inside similar silver envelopes and accompanied by cards whose stygian surfaces were broken only by delicate white letters that told Ben "I am yours. You are mine. Forever." and "I hear your heart. It beats in me. Forever." He'd hidden both of those valentines with the first, never to be touched or even glimpsed by anyone other than himself. The relationship he had with his mystery valentine was sacrosanct. His parents might call it grotesque and inappropriate if they knew; his peers might call it weird and freakish. But to Ben the entire affair was pure miracle, each slash of chalky colored pencil a comet carrying hope that there existed, if only in a disjointed and not entirely corporeal way, someone who might understand him and celebrate his existence without precondition.

This year, though, he hadn't received either card or gift. His Valentine's bag—replete with crude calligraphy, shiny tin-foil moons, and meticulously sketched stars— was utterly barren. Not one classmate had bothered to give him a valentine.

No surprise there.

Ben was becoming accustomed to his classmates' alienation as lonely days stacked one upon another, building a monument to childhood solitude. But, while his bruised ego may have been hardened to Joe DeLucca's repeated wedgies and Andrea Weatherly's name-calling, the sting of his mystery admirer's absence—even if only in the lack of a few obscurely meaningful words and a fleshy trinket—was fresh pain. He didn't need or want love letters—or even "like" letters—from his peers; rather, he yearned after those tidbits of bizarre divinity signed "Forever." This year, there simply wasn't one.

A spitball squished against the nape of Ben's neck. Some boys chuckled.

Ben ignored it all and forced his mind outside, onto a ice-encrusted breeze.

When the principal finally announced the early dismissal and everyone else streamed toward the buses waiting in front of the school, Ben sneaked away, toward the playground. If he was to be lonely, then he wanted to be alone. He could always call his parents and ask them to pick him up later.

Once outside, he clomped around in the snow and stared up into the senseless whorl of tiny crystalline flecks, each an individual soul in this storm, this chaotic, raging blindness that was life. He crumpled to the ground, knees sinking into snowdrifts already a foot deep. Tears flowed across the wind-scoured tundras of his cheeks. Somewhere nearby a vacant swing creaked on rusty chains, singing the serrated melody of isolation.

Ben wiped his eyes with a mittened hand and gazed out over the barren playground.

"Why?" he screamed between barely controlled sobs.

"Why didn't you send me anything? What's wrong with me? What did I do? What's wrong with me? What's wrong with me?"

Bus engines growled in the distance.

Then silence.

Ben sat in the snow for what, to his nine-year-old mind, was hours. The storm continued to strike his face without answer. Eventually, his legs began to go numb.

He rubbed his running nose with the back of his sleeve and stood. There was no reason to stay out in the cold; it couldn't provide any more solace than the warmth inside.

Plodding back to the school, head hung low, Ben didn't expect to see a perfect circle—a cylinder, really—melted into one of the piling snowdrifts by the doors. Yet there it was, a strange little hole, at least a foot in diameter.

Ben stopped, confused, and walked toward it. No footprints led up to its lip or ran away from it. No animal tracks littered the drift.

Approaching cautiously for reasons he couldn't have explained, Ben leaned over the cylindrical hollow, peered to its bottom, and gasped. There, resting on a thin sheen of ice within the hole, was a small black box and, underneath the box, a gleaming silver envelope. Despite the near blizzard-like conditions, snow refused to enter the tiny chasm; here was a place out of time and out of space. Ben reached in and picked up the box and envelope.

He removed his mittens and tore open the envelope. Sure enough, a sable card waited inside. Ghostly words on its face declared "You and I, Ben. You and I. I. You. Us. Us, Ben. Abandoned never. Forever." Ben traced the writing with a finger. He read the card once more, then carefully slid it into the only zippered pocket of his jacket.

Next, the box.

Its design was similar to that of a ring box, with tiny hinges on one of the four sides. Ben flipped up its lid and let out a sound that echoed between the pillars of horror and awe. He didn't drop the box, but came dangerously close.

There, nestled in a perfectly crafted divot within the innocuous cube, Forever stared at Ben; a single eyeball, glistening in translucent liquids and neatly severed from the optic nerve, met his gaze. Its iris was of an uncertain color—perhaps it could best be called gray, though gray was a term far too prosaic to capture the eye's true hue. Flecks of something shining, something vaguely silvery and mirrored, resided in its depths. Ben couldn't tear his vision away from this most recent of gifts. He didn't want to reach out and stroke its moist surface; he just wanted to look at it and know that it was looking back at him.

Minutes evaporated. The wind howled in Ben's ears. In the space between the eyes of the lover and the beloved, all was wondrous serenity.

Uncovered hand aching from subzero breeze, Ben decided to go back inside, find a teacher, and call home. Tonight, snug under the blankets of his bed, he would stare for as long as the moment held him. He snapped the lid shut and skipped into the school, focus never drifting far from the little black cube he held in his hand.

However, what Ben couldn't see was that, once back inside the darkened space of the box, the eye's abysmal pupil had expanded far beyond its bounds and swallowed every last fragment of starry, magical iris.

February 14th, 1994
No one had asked Ben to the Valentine's Day dance. He'd hoped that his lab partner in geology, a slightly

nerdy brunette named Emily Watts, might want to go with him. But someone else—a goateed guy in the grade above them, some sort of guitar player in an amateur grunge band—had taken her instead.

Even though she probably only talked to Ben in class out of necessity and in the hallways between classes out of pity, he liked Emily. He liked the way she made fun of the football team and laughed at the popular kids; he liked the way her hair fell over her right eye when she didn't have it pulled back in a ponytail; he liked the way she smelled of fabric softener and sugar cookies; and he liked that she wore black bras and that, whenever she bent over to examine rock specimens, he could see the mystical place where they ended and her breasts began. He liked so much about her and more. But it was all pointless. She'd wanted to go with that older, cooler, band guy. Ben wasn't even an afterthought.

Yet, filled with a dangerous mixture of unrealistic fantasy and fragile optimism, he came to the dance anyway. He dreamed that maybe Emily would see him there, realize her mistake in coming with the guitar dude, and rush into his arms. So far, it hadn't happened.

From the instant Ben had stepped into the dimly lit gym, he'd squirmed and sweated, trying to find a place to stand that was both unobtrusive but open to invitations from potential dance partners—namely, Emily. Such a place didn't exist, though, and Ben was forced to hover behind the refreshment table. From this vantage point, he watched couples dance; he watched as covert kisses were exchanged when chaperones' faces were turned in adult conversation; he watched hands sliding over curves and into darkened spaces.

The fever of youth sweltered in the gymnasium while he remained frozen, watching.

About an hour after he'd taken up position behind the punch bowl and cookies, Emily and the goateed band guy strolled toward Ben.

Emily waved.

Ben waved back.

They came closer. Too close.

"Hey you," she said.

"Hey," Ben mumbled.

"I didn't expect to see you here. I didn't think this was really your thing."

"Yeah," Ben said, trying to force the quiver from his voice and the redness from his cheeks, "I just thought I should go to one of these for once."

"Yeah. They can be pretty lame. But Anthony wanted to do something with me and I wanted to do something, too. So here we are. You've met Anthony, right?"

She giggled and wrapped an arm around the band guy's—or, more accurately, "Anthony's"—waist.

"Yeah," Ben whispered.

"It's not so bad, really," Emily said, pointing back at the dance floor.

"Yeah, I guess. For some people."

Emily nodded slowly.

Ben swallowed hard.

Uncomfortable silence slid between them.

A breathy love song from the 80s began playing.

Anthony pulled Emily closer.

"You wanna get outta here? Go somewhere else?" he asked, never so much as glancing at Ben.

Emily nodded, beaming.

"See ya later, Benny," she said, turning on her heel and practically skipping across the dance floor, toward the exit.

The two melted into the swirl of shifting bodies.

And that was the end. There was nothing more to do, nothing to say. Emily had made her choice. Tonight she'd make out with the guitar dude, squeeze her hand into his pants and awkwardly tug at what she found inside. By next week, there would probably be more details, more steps. Ben didn't want to imagine any of it—the laughter, the slicked skin, the not-quite words, the lapping motions —but he was forced to.

He opened his eyes wide, as wide as he possibly could, and let visions of the dance rush in. Flowing dresses, shiny ties, shuffling feet, and the spiraling nebulae of disco ball reflections—these were at the blurry center of Ben's concentration. If he could fill his mind with enough random imagery, enough non-sequitur thoughts, then perhaps the hellish vacancy that drew tortures inside his head would be crowded out.

He needed to leave. He needed to go home and watch TV or play Super Mario World. Mindless distraction was a whore who would always take him into her outstretched arms.

Ben shrugged himself to action. He walked out of the gym, turned down a hallway, and found one of the school's two payphones. He called his parents and asked them to pick him up. They didn't ask why. He hung up and stood in the empty hall, hand on the receiver. Muffled, dying beats pulsed in the air. Whether they originated in the chambers of his heart or the cavern of the gymnasium, he couldn't be sure.

All day, Ben had been focused on only one thing: Emily. He dreamed about their night together, their first dance, and the way she'd feel pressed against his chest. He'd barely even given thought to the fact that, when he'd left his house earlier in the evening, his yearly Valentine hadn't arrived yet. Now, he regretted his decision to stray from the lonely companionship Forever's promise offered.

Ben wandered away from the phone, shuffling through the shadows of an unlit passage that led to the library. It would take his parents at least fifteen or twenty minutes to drive to the school; in the meantime, he could simply merge with darkness.

As he made his way along the hall he rapped his knuckles against the row of lockers that stood to one side of the narrow corridor. He held some vague apprehension that someone might knock back from the other side.

No one did.

He continued on.

With his gaze fastened to the floor, Ben turned a few corners and found himself standing before the entrance to the library. Oddly, one of the doors was ajar and a light—apparently near the end of its glaring, fluorescent life—was spastically flickering somewhere deeper inside.

Ben was drawn toward its incomprehensible pattern.

He crept into the library foyer, straining for silence in his footfalls. The harsh light blinked out its schizophrenic S.O.S. from a private study room to his left. Though his hands began to sweat and his knees felt wobbly, he kept inching closer to the light, pulled forward as if on ethereal strings. Before he consciously realized that he had reached his destination, Ben found himself standing in front of the study room's door, pressing his face to its tiny rectangular window. Inside, he saw the package and the envelope, neatly arranged on a table.

He opened the door as one might open the door to an execution chamber or a cathedral—reverently, carefully, making sure not to be too eager for fear something with the power to crush bodies and souls might be offended or, worse yet, might flee into the sky and be eternally un-known. Stepping into the small study room, Ben smelled an aroma he couldn't place—a potent mixture of citrus and sulfur, perhaps. As it dissipated into the learned hollows of the library, his interest in the odor's unusual composition waned and he focused on his tangible gifts.

First, the letter.

He grabbed it from off the table, carefully slid his finger under the flap, and tore an opening across the top. Pulling the card from within, he saw more dream-scribbled words than ever before. The card read: "Ben. You hurt. You will always hurt and be hurt. By them. By them all. But I am with you. I need you. Without reserve. Without hesitation. Hold me. Caress me. You are mine. I am yours. We. We. We. Forever."

Ben's hand shook. His stomach churned, not un-pleasantly. He wanted to climb between the lines on the card and snuggle there, never to return to the world of dances and Emilys and abrupt, awkward goodbyes. He'd made a terrible mistake in taking for granted that Forever would still be waiting for him, regardless of whether a relationship with Emily worked out or not.

After a series of deep breaths, he scooped up the package—a small, rectangular box that in a more con-ventional universe might have held a necklace or bracelet —and removed its lid. Hidden away inside, lying on a bed of black velvet, was a pair of plump, rosy lips.

Ben brought them close to his face. They were perfect. Each one turned up at its edges ever so slightly, drawing what may have once been an arc of pleasure or sin. A delicious sheen of gloss covered their surface and reflected the flickering light. Ben knew what was about to happen; waves crashed and ebbed within his abdomen. His hands, as if not his own, pushed the box toward his waiting mouth.

Lips touched lips. Somewhere far beyond the reaches of satellites and telescopes, a segment of space and time cracked and fell away. This was Ben's first kiss, his only kiss. A kiss from Forever.

For a moment, only a moment, Ben wondered if Emily's lips tasted as deliciously tart, as full of possibility and passion as those in the box. He wondered if any girl could be as amazing as the girl he was already with, the girl he wasn't with at all.

For a moment, he considered the strangeness of his love, then he kissed the warm, welcoming lips again.

February 14th, 1998

By the time he was a senior in high school, Ben was beginning to suspect that the grotesque Valentines were a practical joke perpetrated by someone he'd known for years. He was sure that the various body parts, while convincingly well-made, were latex or some other synthetic material. After all, in twelve years none of them had shriveled or rotted away. Though he was by no means an expert on the subject of death and decay, he understood enough about biological processes to realize that, unless these human remains had been expertly embalmed, there was no logical way that they could have remained in the same soft, smooth state for so long. Their longevity supported his malignant suspicions. The fact that they were perpetually warm was more problematic.

Ben had reasoned that the parts must have been composed of some sort of exothermic material, a strange polymer used for space vehicles or something. He had no solid idea on that front, only inexact theories that seemed to fill the holes in reality.

The envelopes and the packages had continued to arrive like clockwork, every year another piece, every year another remarkable fabrication. Ben had no clue as to who would be willing to put so much time, money, and effort into screwing with him, though. He couldn't fathom anyone caring enough about him to invest their energies in the Valentines—a potential strike against his theory.

Of course, regardless of whether the parts were real or not, he still wasn't willing to throw them in the trash; there was, in some intangible yet crucial way, a disingenuous sparkle in the rationalization of their origins, as if a brilliant light had burst into existence only to reveal the vastness of a much richer darkness.

Today, Ben was skipping school because he wanted to capture the truth that he believed existed. He wanted to witness the moment of Valentine delivery—the conception of what, for so many years, he had felt was a miracle. He was sure that if he simply sequestered himself inside his room and set up a video cameras at the front and back doors of the house, he could capture evidence of the trickery or, at very least, learn the hidden identity of the gift giver. Today would be the day he uncloaked mystery.

Lying on his bed, waiting for he knew not what, Ben cranked up the volume on one of his Nine Inch Nails CDs and stared at the ceiling. A spiked weight seemed to press up from behind his back, arching along his spine. It was the gifts. They needed contact.

He hadn't kissed the lips in months, and he hadn't touched any of the other parts in even longer; they remained imprisoned in a dusty fire-safe under a loose board beneath his bed. His hands ached to free them, to knead them, to either possess them or be possessed by them. Beads of sweat began to form on his forehead. He wouldn't reach down and pry up the board. He wouldn't. He had fought these urges before and he'd fight them this time as well. His heart raced; all motion ceased. The whole of the universe was here, in his room, in the struggle to deny desire. He had to hold out for one more day.

Only one more day.

By tomorrow, he'd know whether he should lay his offerings on reason's alter or kneel to the throb and pulse rebounding along every fibrous pathway in his body.

Ben swung himself out of bed and wandered away from his room. His parents were at work. Even though he had the house to himself, he felt as if a thousand eyes were trained on his every twitch.

"I'm going to find you today!" he shouted.

"I'm going to make you show me your face! I need to see your face!"

He didn't expect a reply and he didn't receive one.

Outside, a car alarm was chirping like the spawn of hellbound sparrows and mechanical bees.

Ben walked to the living room, turned on the television, and hit the mute button. So far, everything was normal.

Two hours later, he was still seated in front of the TV, half asleep. A rerun of Seinfeld babbled silently in the background. He hadn't heard a single creak of a board from the patio out back or any shuffle of feet on the brick pathway to the front door. Two hours for nothing. His parents wouldn't be home until well after eight o'clock, though, so there was still plenty of time left to keep vigil.

Ben stretched and yawned. Debunking the paranormal was a tedious affair.

Groaning, he struggled free from his family's miasmic couch and walked to the computer in his father's office. It was on. It was always on, a luminous beacon of dead communication. He plopped into a creaky maple chair—his parents loved antiques—and connected to the internet. The dial-up modem squealed to its brethren. Soon, he was drowning in a sea of information and the "real" world—whatever that might be—melted away.

Another two hours passed into ephemera.

Mid-afternoon now.

A perfunctory check of the patio and the front stoop revealed nothing. Ben wrung his hands. Patience was his virtue, but worry was his vice. If he didn't catch the Valentines' sender he'd remain suspended between the scissoring blades of desire and reason for another full year. He simply couldn't hold out that long. It was impossible.

Sometimes, deep within the trenches of night, he

swore that he heard the lips whispering his name. Sometimes he'd find himself ensconced in a daydream, silently mouthing the word "Forever." It seemed that incorporeal chains were fastened between himself and the objects in the box under his bed, and they could only be broken by incontrovertible evidence of banality or deceit. Perhaps not even then.

Ben sighed, trudged to the kitchen, and made a peanut butter sandwich.

He wasted another hour playing video games then tried to masturbate without imagining the dotted outline of a fragmentary woman, her features and forms endlessly spinning through sweating space. He couldn't. He needed her fantastic indeterminability just to remain hard.

Another hour died from inactivity. It was now late afternoon and twilight stars were beginning to invade the sky. Still no sign of visitation at either doors or windows. Ben was beginning to wonder if his plan had been discovered. Was it possible that the Valentines' gifter had been monitoring his poor excuse for a stakeout (or, in this case, stakein) and laughing at his lackadaisical vigilance all along?

Back on the couch after his self-gratification, he punched a cushion and swore. Outside, a trio of boys rode by on bicycles. They made loud noises steeped in furious argument or gleeful abandon; it was impossible to discern which was the case.

Ben pulled at his hair and murmured "Why won't you come? Why won't you come when I'm looking?"

The questions fell to the floor, ignored. Even silence refused to answer.

Evening wore on and darkness seeped through the windows. Ben paced between the living room and the kitchen. How was he supposed to disprove the mystical if he couldn't prove the mundane? His brilliant plan was crumbling. Nothing wasn't supposed to happen.

"Goddamn it!" Ben screamed, kicking over a stool in the kitchen.

"Just show yourself! Just show yourself for once!" he cried.

He ran out the back door, hopped off the patio, and, in an act of prostration to the gods of frustration and defeat, was about to throw himself down in the middle of his family's lush, fenced-in lawn when a twitch of movement in the corner of his eye arrested the entire ceremony. He froze.

It was probably just a cat, but hope springs eternal in places light cannot touch.

Ben turned slowly and peered into the shadows at the corner of the house where he thought he'd seen motion. He crept forward, hands balled into fists.

As he neared the Maginot Line where celestial glimmer met cimmerian pitch, a rat darted out from beside the house; it scampered by mere inches from Ben's feet. This was neither the sadistic prankster nor the divine messenger for whom he had hoped. This was the stilettoed laugh of the absurdly ordinary. He kicked the ground and swore.

His parents would be home in less than two hours. The plan had truly failed.

Ben trudged back inside, locked the screen leading to the patio, and, with stale gaze and sullen steps, made his way upstairs to his room. As he opened the door to his increasingly embattled domain, a blast of torpid air rolled out. Its odor—sulfuric, with a hint of something pleasantly unnameable—was familiar. He had experienced this smell before, though he wasn't immediately certain when or where. The memory flashed, a pop of light, a mirrored shimmer, then was gone.

He stepped into his room.

The skepticism that had been amassing armies in his chest suddenly fell to tatters under a sharp rain of unabashed wonder. Somehow, someway, lying atop his bed were a black envelope and an ornate, sliver, hexagonal box.

Without thinking, Ben ran to the front door. It remained locked. He ran to each and every window on the first floor of the house. Locked, locked, locked, locked; they were all locked tight. He jogged back upstairs and stared at the Valentine. It was impossible. He had been outside for less than five minutes. No one could have broken in, sneaked to his room, left the gifts, and fled without a trace in so little time. Impossible. Unless, of course, the perpetrator was still in the house. It was a clichéd conclusion, but it was also the last bastion of logic.

Ben raced around the house, moving from closet to closet, flinging doors wide open; he shined flashlights under furniture; he even searched inside particularly expansive cabinets. He found no one. A crazy, zig-zagging fissure was beginning to split his mind. There was no one in the house—no one that could've ever been in the house—and yet the Valentine was lying upon his bed, yearning to be taken into his hands. Reason did not complement reality. Ben sprinted back to his room. Though his head was collapsing, his pulse had never beaten stronger or with more urgency.

Once inside his room again, he knelt beside his bed and gently tore one side from the black envelope. The card within—a constant unflinching as entropy—read:

"Ben. You doubt me. You doubt us. You mustn't. You must believe. Together we fill the void. Together we are the answers. Together, Ben. Only together. Forever."

She knew. She knew him. She knew him too well. His confusion, his trepidation, his newfound faith in gods that could be poked and prodded, measured and verified: these were the magicks she sought to dispel with her words and her flesh.

Ben delicately placed the card back on the bed and reached for the ornate silver hexagon. Its top and sides were engraved with obscure glyphs, some of which vaguely resembled mathematical symbols. A few were reminiscent of Cyrillic letters. Neither comparison was accurate, though; there was something wrong with these marks, something Ben couldn't quite comprehend. If he had to explain what was strange about these glyphs, he would have stammered something about them feeling too heavy. A length of meaning, interminable and chaotic, seemed to stretch out behind each of the tiny, arcane symbols. Ben began to trace several with his finger. As he worked along their sharp angles, a crushing weight descended upon his chest and a roiling, churning river of images burst into his mind just below his consciousness. His breath and his thoughts were subsumed by an endless vista of potentiality. He was drowning.

Resisting on instinct alone, Ben dropped his hand from the gaudy container. He gasped for blessed oxygen.

He couldn't imagine what rested inside the box if the

box itself was so powerful, so overwhelming. Minutes ticked by. He didn't want to see or hold the object within the metallic hexagon, but, at the same time, all he wanted to do was see and hold it. Ben was facing himself in a standoff at high noon. No matter what choices he made, he would be both the loser and the winner, the hero and the villain, the dead and the living.

With palms sweating and chilled, he summoned a lax, flabby sort of courage and, in one quick flick of the wrist, flipped up the box's lid. Glancing over its rim, he bore witness to the box's contents. A gasp trickled from the corner of his mouth. There, resting on what seemed to be a silk interior, was a glistening, throbbing heart roughly the size of his fist. It pumped no blood. It fed no vital stream. It was not connected to any tangible system of electrical impulses and cellular directives. And yet it beat. Impossible, unless Forever was more than a fiction, more than mischief and hoax.

Ben reached in and picked up the heart. Its expansion and contraction did not falter; in fact—though it may have been entirely imaginary—he sensed a quickening of its pulse.

His hands slick with the clear, viscous fluid that covered the entire organ, Ben peered into one of its severed arteries. He saw nothing but striated muscle and space. No battery pack ran this object; no tendrils of wire snaked through its pulpy interior. He turned it over and over again, examining it from every angle, but found only more unbroken, pumping flesh. No forgery, not even those produced by Hollywood wizards, could match the intricacy of the instrument in his hands.

He laughed, a bellowing, whipping rain of manic

mirth. All sense slid away, all logic fled in horror. They were no longer of use to him, anyway. The fissure that had been forming inside his head tore wide open, metastasizing into a fathomless chasm that pulsed in time with the beating of the heart in his hands. Glee, thoughtless, wicked glee, flew screeching from its depths. Ben brought the heart to his mouth and kissed it. With the tip of his tongue, he tickled the rims of each stunted artery and vein. Strings of liquid drizzled off his chin.

Forever had given him a sign. Forever had given him her heart. He had been a fool to doubt.

He knew that tonight, for the first time in many nights, he'd pull the safe out from under the floorboard and cradle it in his arms as he slept.

At such thoughts, the heart in his hands beat ever faster, ever hungrier.

February 14th, 2000

His dorm room was swathed in black fabric. Black sheets, black blankets, a black carpet, black towels hanging on a silver rod, black jacket draped over a black chair. A particle hewn from the fabric of twilight orbited every atom in the room.

Ben sat on his bed, reading Kierkegaard's Philosophical Fragments. Unlike many of the people he'd met in his classes, his interest in philosophy wasn't pure posturing. He didn't read Nietzsche so he could justify his youthful angst and he didn't memorize lines of Sartre so that he could wax intellectual with the arty kids who smoked clove cigarettes in the dorm lounge. Rather, he loved philosophy because it fashioned a slim doorway to abstraction. It granted him moments of reprieve from the solid, too-sharply defined world, moments in which he could wade in contemplative formlessness. Ideas didn't require substance or volume; they merely required someone to believe. Ben found solace in this controlled ephemerality.

Tonight, though, he was unable to lose himself in the intricate thoughts of dead men because tonight was both a Friday and Valentine's Day.

Certainly, either occasion would have been sufficient reason for mass bacchanalia on a university campus but, combined, the possibilities were endless. Ben had seen flyers that promoted lingerie parties, foam parties, costume parties, pimp-and-ho parties, and ever-popular but relatively pedestrian keggers. Most of the festivities were held off-campus or in Greek housing, but a daring few—utterly disregarding university policy—had been organized in dorms. Ben was well aware of the existence of these covert bashes, since his neighbors across the hallway were throwing one.

He hadn't been invited.

Actually, he'd never even spoken to his neighbor across the hall—a pug-nosed blonde guy who rarely wore a shirt and tended to yell incoherent monosyllables like "woo" and "yah" when he was drunk, which, as it happened, was more than half of any given week.

Ben shook his head and rubbed his temples.

Bass beats exploded against the walls of his room; the thrum of conversation corkscrewed into his ears; an acid current drifted under his door and crawled upon his skin, burning and laughing. He simply couldn't focus on the impalpable with a sweating, bellowing, fecund mass so near his hallowed space.

Someone stumbled against his door, smashing an elbow or a knee into unyielding wood. Epithets were screamed; mindless guffaws followed. Bass continued to pound.

Ben snapped shut his book and sighed. The idiots across the hallway were misunderstanding the holiday. Romance was an atomic whisper, not an empty roar. He just wanted some quiet time, a few hours spent reading and a few hours spent with Forever, but the party was a distraction he couldn't easily ignore. He hoped that its attendees would soon tire of the cramped spaces of a dorm room and wander into the night in search of less constraining debaucheries. After all, he had big plans.

Earlier in the day, after his newest Valentine's gift had arrived and he had realized its full implications, Ben ran to the on-campus general store and bought a box of chocolates and two scented candles. He wanted to find a bottle of wine, too, but he had no social connections that would allow for underage drinking. The candy and ambient lighting would have to do. He'd also considered purchasing a box of condoms, but didn't really see any point—conception was clearly out of the question and disease was a distant concern.

He couldn't, or perhaps wouldn't, envision Forever's nether regions as a flowering infirmary. The very notion was blasphemy.

Outside, glass shattered, instantly producing a compound of shrieks and chortles.

This wasn't how he had dreamed the evening would play out. He'd pictured stellar vistas overhead and a downy pile of blankets beneath, passages of Hegel or Schopenhauer read aloud and long draughts of flowing carmine. He'd pictured laughter and hushed secrets, revealed only in the union of lips and moist flesh. He'd pictured no one else within miles. But pictures were, unfortunately, only approximations of reality. If Ben was to lose his virginity tonight, it would be without starshine and glaze.

He reached under his pillow and withdrew a small, polished obsidian box. His fingers glided easily across its surface and over its rounded corners and edges. A tremor, a roseate wave of heat, perpetually oscillated about its perimeter. And yet it was only a transport, a vessel in which ecstasy, its lone passenger, had traversed unknown distances. Inside was the fear-inducer, the leveler of kingdoms, the meatus of God's scorn and man's delight. With chilled, tremulous hands, he removed the box's top and tried to let the party next door dissolve into meaningless white noise.

But it wouldn't. The polyphonic orgy did not hush for his special moment.

A tiny, viperous area of Ben's brain began to squirm. The party across the hall was unacceptable. Tonight had to retain some petty semblance of perfection.

He leaped off the bed and strode to the door. He had no blueprint for quieting his neighbors, no vengeful mousetrap to set before them. His hands balled into fists, he halted and considered what he might be able to accomplish by marching across the hall. He knew he wouldn't have the bravado to confront anyone. His stomach twisted at simple, casual greetings; asking for—or better yet, demanding—silence from a virtual stranger was beyond the scope of his social powers.

What could he do? What could he possibly do? He was failing Forever.

In her card this year, she'd written: "Ben. You and I are alone. Always alone together. Always together alone. Make sure we're alone. Tonight. Tonight we rend galaxies with the force of our love. But only alone and in quietus, Ben. Only alone and in quietus. Forever."

He couldn't give her the solitude or the stillness she deserved—not with a party raging seven feet away. No immediate resolution presented itself. How could this be his night of satin dreams? How could this be his indoctrination into the secret order of the sexually initiated? How could he be so impotent?

Bass continued to pound and inchoate voices continued to rise and fall. Someone began singing Beethoven's Ode to Joy, replacing all the lyrics with one repeated phrase: "My cock."

Ben screamed and threw a punch at the door. It slammed in time to one of the throbbing beats. He drew back and smashed his fist against unforgiving oak again and again, matching the pulse outside. His knuckles split open and bled, and still he pounded the door. Bone cracked, splintered. Wood slivered into gaping wounds. Still, he pounded.

Pain forced time to curve inward, upon itself. Ben hit the door for what may have been minutes or millennia.

Finally, the singing stopped. Feminine laughter tickled the air. The bass continued pumping at full volume.

Ben slumped, panting, onto the floor. The door was beautifully spattered and oozing, a post-modern hybrid of Jackson Pollock and Edgar Allen Poe. His hand had worked artistry; unfortunately, it had also been tenderized in the process. It lay on his lap in a pile of crimson rivulets and fleshy flecks. Two of his knuckles—both entirely stripped of skin—were chipped and broken. They sparkled in the dim yellow light of his reading lamp.

A tiny, feathered part of Ben's brain chirruped for medical attention but it was drowned in the blissful wash of emptiness that swept over him. He was soiled and spent and, oddly enough, satisfied.

The bass continued to hammer at the door and he didn't care. Something had changed. Something had either died or been born. Perhaps both.

Exhausted, Ben crawled to his bed, rolled himself upon it, and fell into a sleep reserved only for gladiators, mystics, and lovers.

Two nights later, after his hand had been sutured and set, Ben would unzip his fly and enter the deep, damp, rubicund realms of which he'd fantasized. He would be overcome with pleasure, with joy, and with a sense of gratification unlike any other he'd ever experienced. And yet, whenever he recalled the sequence of events in the months and years to come, he always felt that the night he'd mutilated his hand was truly the night he had lost his virginity.

February 14th, 2004
A FedEx truck pulled up in front of Ben's apartment,

the bottom floor of a fading duplex home. He knew the truck would be arriving today and he knew what it would be bringing, so he'd called in sick to work earlier that morning. The bookstore could manage itself without him for one day.

As the deliveryman descended the stairs of his vehicle, Ben glanced at a list on the coffee table, a compilation of everything that Forever had sent him since he was six years old. It included, itemized by year:

1986—1 finger (possibly ring or index)

1987—6 teeth (2 canines, 4 molars)

1988—1 ear, left

1989—1 eye (silver-gray iris)

1990—1 hand, right, all digits intact (entirely without
        fingerprints, as if horribly burned)

1991—1 eye (also silver-gray iris)

1992—1 nose, small & scrunched

1993—1 arm, right, without hand

1994—2 lips (soft, pink, and full)

1995—1 tongue

1996—1 ear, right

1997—10 teeth (assorted—of all types)

1998—1 heart (perpetually beating)

1999—1 coil of intestine, approx. 2' in length

2000—1 vagina

2001—2 breasts (one medium size—B cup? one larger—
        C or D cup?)

2002—1 circle of skin, approx. 6" in diameter (pale, hairless,
        smooth)

2003—2 strips of skin, 1' foot in length, 8" width (same
        smoothness as previous skin, but with olive
        complexion)

Ben smiled and patted the sheet of paper upon which he'd scrawled the list. This was his girl. His Forever.

Despite the cultural pervasiveness of advice from faux gurus and pop psychologists, he'd reached the conclusion that he didn't need anyone else. He no longer held any illusions of relationships with "real" women. He was, after all, twenty-four years old and he'd never been on a date; he'd never caressed, kissed, or made love to a "real" woman. He could barely speak to them. In truth, he could barely speak to anyone.

His was a life of internal dialogues and dynamic inactivities. He talked to himself, he talked to Forever, and he talked to his parents. His interactions with co-workers were brief, formal, and often garnished with forced smiles and feigned platitudes. Friends were a long-extinct concept. Occasionally, he called phone sex hot-lines and asked the women on the other end to recite Forever's letters but, for the most part, his social sphere was flat. He didn't mind.

He peered through the window again.

The FedEx deliveryman was struggling to unload a tall wooden crate, Ben's package, the reason he was skipping work.

Ben laughed. He wondered whether the deliveryman could have guessed at what was in the crate. Probably. Only a fool wouldn't realize the truth that, day after day, he was chauffeuring sublime perversities from the twisting corners of the earth to the main street of Everytown, America. The contents of Ben's crate were assuredly no more shocking than many others.

The doorbell rang.

Ben jumped toward the door, eager to have his new

possession.

The deliveryman stood on the threshold, an electronic pad in hand and the crate on a dolly beside him. He glanced at Ben.

"Benjamin Apple?"

Ben nodded. The FedEx man held out the pad and Ben signed quickly. He dove at the package and, with a few grunts and popping joints, hefted it off the dolly and slid it into the apartment. He muttered some polite trans-actional nonsense in the deliveryman's direction, then stepped back inside and closed the door. He jogged to the kitchen, fished in a drawer for a hammer, and returned to the crate.

A few hurried hacks and tugs later, one of the sides fell from the massive box in a tidal wave of packing peanuts. Ben waded through the styrofoam sea and pulled a limp, frigid body from its clutches. He carried it to his couch and laid it down carefully.

She was beautiful.

Even without eyes, without lips, without breasts or an unbroken covering of skin, she was beautiful.

Ben gawked at the craftsmanship of her form, the smooth, naked concavities and the snowy, gentle swells. She was exactly as he'd imagined, exactly as he'd specified when he ordered her.

He pinched her underarm, testing the texture and elasticity of her flesh. Despite the fact that it was some sort of composite substance made from rubber and silicone, it flexed and bunched easily between his fingers, firm yet supple. Science in service of pleasure was truly a remarkable thing.

Ben sat at the foot of the sex toy, counting its dismemberments, checking to ensure that the manufacturer had sheared or uninstalled all the proper parts. There were, of course, no eyes, lips, or breasts; he'd already seen as much. The doll, as per his request, also lacked ears, a nose, a right arm, a finger on its left hand, and a wide swath of skin on its stomach.

He ran a finger up between its legs and felt nothing. No silky falseness resided there, no soft mockery. Just emptiness, as he had specified.

He clapped his hands and laughed. The doll was perfect. Or, more pointedly, it would be perfect once he had glued and stapled and stitched in all the pieces of Forever.

It had taken nearly a year to find a company that would create this radiant abomination. Most manufacturers had said that their molding process didn't allow for such construction; a few had told Ben, in congenial language, that they didn't cater to disfigurement fetishists; some didn't even bother to reply to his queries.

He'd taken it all in stride, confident that someone with the right technology would recognize that his need was not for the lack but for the possibilities that the lack offered. Tru-Woman, LLC, of Poughkeepsie, New York, had done just that. They had made his doll, no unnecessary questions asked and no moral fright exhibited. He was so thankful that he considered sending the sales reps at Tru-Woman a fruit basket, though, eventually, decided that the eight thousand dollars they'd charged his credit card was probably repayment enough.

Ben patted the doll's thigh and exited to his bedroom, just a few steps away. A minute later, he reentered the living room carrying two increasingly cramped fire safes and a cardboard box full of crafting supplies. He unlocked one of the safes and removed an alabaster sheet of skin. Lovingly, he raised the flesh to his nose and inhaled the tart, smoky aroma he'd come to associate with Forever. An involuntary shiver cascaded up his arms and down his spine.

Freeing himself from the moment, he kneeled before the doll and lowered the patch of flesh over one of its exposed plastic surfaces. It blended with the surrounding rubber-silicone surface almost seamlessly. Had Ben not been able to see the faint line running about the skin's perimeter, he would have had no idea where the illusion stopped and the authentic began.

He bent over and kissed the flesh, then turned his face to the side and licked the doll. Again, he kissed flesh and licked doll. The binary had already fused in his mind.

He backed away from his project and dumped the box of crafting supplies on the floor. Glue guns, staple guns, tacks, pins, epoxies, needles, thread, scissors: a small hobby or scrapbooking store spilled out. Ben nodded to himself and to the gods of innovation. It was time to piece together a puzzle. It was time to make a woman.

February 14, 2008

For the first and only time, the silver envelope arrived without an accompanying package. The midnight card inside was inscribed with just eight simple words: "Next year. I'm coming. For you. Finally. Forever."

Having just read the card, Ben was slumped on the floor, gripping his chest. His heart was striking a joyous eleventh hour. Through raging pulse, he wondered: Can this mean what it says? A year? Only one more year? Twenty-two gone. Twenty-two spent waiting and wondering. But now? Now the sacrifice will pay off.

He would have called someone to regale with the good news, but his cell phone held only three numbers: his parents' home, the store where he worked, and an emergency contact which, as it happened, was also his parents' home. He had no one with which to share his delight. It might have been for the best. Who would understand his love, anyway? Who could be excited for his piecemeal bride?

Ben leaped to his feet and strolled to his bedroom with one desire: to kiss the lips that promised a future and to revel in the lost organs that might soon rejoin their owner.

February 14th, 2008 was the happiest day in Ben's truncated life. He never left his apartment. He barely left his bedroom.

February 14th, 2009

Sporting a new haircut and a new suit, Ben sat at the breakfast bar in his apartment and stared at a pair of fluttering cardinals beyond the kitchen window. He wondered what time the doorbell would ring. The sun was sagging just above the horizon, well on its descent to oblivion. Night would soon leap from the ceiling and the floor and sharpen the blades of anticipation that had already been slicing across Ben's throat for hours. He fidgeted and tugged at his tie.

One of the cardinals slammed against the window and disappeared. It may have glided, exuberant and swelling with dervish energy, back into the hyaline vista above or it may have landed, cracked and twisted, in a scarlet lump beneath the pane. In either case, Ben didn't notice.

He jumped off the stool upon which he had been perched and began pacing between his kitchen and his living room—a space of ten or fifteen feet, just enough room to cultivate distress. A platinum chain necklace he'd bought for Forever the day before bounced around inside one of his pockets, smacking time against his thigh and coiling upon itself. Every step brought another strike of the hidden metronome.

Trying to smooth over his bunching anxieties, Ben walked to his tiny dinner table and set about subtly rearranging its contents. He'd been proud of his decorating skills when he'd set up the table an hour ago, but now he saw only failure and disarray. He yanked at the black table cloth, moved the pair of candles closer to the center, slid the sparkling silverware away from the plates one inch, took the candles off the table entirely, pushed the silverware back to its original position, then placed the candles back on the table. He sighed and gingerly sank into one of the fragile wicker chairs that had come free with the table. Waiting was always most difficult the second before it ended.

Ben fished the necklace from his pocket and laid it on the table. Clasped, it had no definite beginning or end; it simply wound in loops of infinite glitter, curves of forever. Forever for Forever. Ben snorted, a half-laugh for a joke that didn't really exist. He rose and shuffled to the couch. Television was a faithful anesthetic and he needed an injection—something, anything, to calm his nerves. He plopped down, hit "Power" on his remote, and let himself drift into a different sort of limbo. Somehow, he felt that this day wasn't as different from all the others as he'd hoped.

Five hours later, waist-deep in a History Channel marathon on the Dark Ages, Ben began to contemplate the possibility that Forever might not arrive. His suit was starting to wrinkle and the dinner he'd planned— microwaveable fettuccine alfredo and frozen, precooked chicken piccata—was long since thawed. Outside, heavy sleet was rebounding off every hard surface it struck; it had been falling steadily for at least forty-five minutes, so the roads were surely encased in a shell of ice by now. He wondered what he'd do if the night passed without Forever. Would he continue on, making love to the woman-doll and envisioning a translucent day when she would hold him as tightly as he held her? Or would he surrender and chug a bottle of bleach? He wasn't sure. Luckily, he didn't have to make the decision, because, as he was imagining what vomiting one's own dissolving esophagus and stomach must feel like, the power in his apartment suddenly went out.

Unexpected silence and darkness crashed against the walls.

Ben didn't stir. He sat on the couch and waited for the electricity to surge through whatever natural force had blocked its way.

A minute passed.

Then two.

Silence and darkness still held control. Whatever failure had occurred must have been widespread, because even the streetlamps outside had faded to black.

Ben rose with a grunt, stumbled to the kitchen, and found a pack of matches lying beside the sink—a remnant of his morning preparations. Earlier, when he had set the table, he'd lit the candles and let them burn for just a few seconds so that, when Forever finally arrived and it was time for dinner, all the wax would be stripped from their wicks and they'd ignite without any embarrassing fumbling. His fastidious planning had made everything so desperately perfect, so painfully charming. But now it would be all for naught. The spread had to be disassembled in service of utility.

With a sigh, Ben grabbed the candles from off the table and lit each in turn. They accepted the flame without the slightest hesitation. One he plunked down on the breakfast bar and the other he kept with him. He carried it, crystal holder and all, back into the living room, eventually setting it atop a small table beside the couch. Sleet continued to ping and thunk against the windows and the roof.

Ben stared upward, wondering how loud the noise must have been in the unyielding hollows of the vacant apartment above his own. It was as if the sky was trying to beat down the arrogance of all things that might dare stretch toward its invisible paradises. He shrugged away such thoughts and returned to his sedentary detention upon the couch.

As he waited in the relative darkness, hands clasped tightly between his legs, he heard something between the pings and thunks of sleet—a soft sound, a hissed rubbing, of fabric against fabric or palm against palm, perhaps. Moving in sinuous, elastic arcs, it slithered easily into his ear. He held his breath and strained his concentration, but couldn't quite determine its source over the ambient din of the storm; the sound seemed to be nowhere more specific than "in the air." Ice, hurled ever more wildly by its harsh masters in the firmament above, pounded the roof with increasing urgency and force. The onslaught momentarily drowned out the hiss. However, it couldn't mask the heavy thud that suddenly issued from Ben's bedroom.

Ben jumped and instinctively clutched at the couch's armrest. As he stared at the doorway anticipating an in-definite something to happen, he began to smell it—the sulfur, the citrus, the smoke and the dreams. Forever. He leaped off the couch, snatched the candle from the table beside him, and ran to the bedroom.

Halfway to the threshold, though, he stopped, immobile and stricken with a feeling of excited dread. There, before him, crawling one-armed through his bedroom doorway, was the Tru-Woman doll, naked and silent. It propelled itself as a caterpillar might, pulling itself forward with its living, Forever-given arm while arching its back and dragging its rubbery legs up to meet the rest of its body.

Ben gasped.

He wanted to pick up the doll—if it was, in fact, his Forever—and kiss her, but he couldn't. Its motion was so unsettling, so alien, that some base self-preservation instinct, an ancient primate fear, wouldn't let him step any closer.

The doll wormed forward and Ben remained stationary. He couldn't see its face, as its head hung, pendulous and limp, from its shoulders. Polished black hair and shadow occluded any view of its visage beyond the gentle line of its lower jaw.

Now only five or six feet away from Ben—nearly within his reach—the doll stopped, propping itself up on its one animated arm.

Ben held his breath.

Slowly, the doll lowered itself to the floor, face down. Once lying flat and still, its arm grabbed a clump of raven hair and pulled back, so that its head rested upon its chin. Ben crouched and, hand quivering, held the candle out before him. Forever's silvery eyes rolled up to meet his gaze. For the first time, he felt that she was looking at him as he had always looked at her.

And then she smiled.

The embers of warmth in Ben's heart exploded. He couldn't breathe; he couldn't move; he couldn't think or feel anything other than an atomic wall of fire rolling through his being, incinerating every part of his body, mind, and soul. Spectral flames consumed him from the inside out. He opened his mouth to scream, but only air escaped his lungs. If this was love, it was all the love in the universe, condensed and concentrated into one dense, unforgiving point. It was the grip of God. It was the rack of hell.

Ben collapsed on the floor and dropped his candle, which rolled under a nearby chair and winked out. He glanced up at the doll, at Forever, at whatever she or it was. In the dim light he could still see that its smile, coy and self-satisfied, held firm. He reached out, groping for the Forever-doll's touch, but it remained just out of reach. It simply laid on the floor, bemusedly watching him struggle with this, its final gift.

Through the burning, through the undiluted passion and intensity of ultimate experience, Ben heard his front door burst open. He couldn't imagine what was coming next. Grinding his teeth in an effort to fighting back the boiling euphoria inside him, Ben rolled onto his back. Something was shuffling across the room, something that smelled even more sulfuric, even more tartly acidic than the Forever-doll. He could sense it coming, feet dragging, closer and closer.

A blast of superheated wind rushed over his face. In its currents he heard what sounded like millions of overlapping voices all speaking in tandem, as one singular voice. Some masculine baritones and basses lined its lower registers, but, for the most part, the voice was composed of sultry female tones—bedroom whispers of a sort. It repeated only one word: "Benjamin. Benjamin. Benjamin."

Another blast of wind swept over Ben, and in the wind, more words: "I am here. For you."

The shuffling thing was closing rapidly and had reached the Forever-doll. Ben tried to sit up, but the intensity of feeling was too much. He could do no more than turn his head to see the thing's vague form in the flickering light of the kitchen candle. It seemed to have no specific shape, but, rather, was constantly expanding and shrinking, developing and erasing. What looked like a head melted away and was replaced by what might have been a hand; legs dissolved into its mid-section and were replaced by elongated elbows.

Ben was grateful that he couldn't see any more specific features.

"Forever?" he groaned through the pleasure-pain.

The hot wind whipped against his face.

"Forever, Ben. Together. Soon," it answered.

Ben might have wanted to tell this thing—this living manifestation of incoherence—that he'd waited his entire life for her and that she was his destiny, but he couldn't separate his own emotions from the inferno of passion continually pressing deeper inside him. He could feel nothing and think nothing but love. Supreme love. Total love. The kind of love that ignites murders of passion, the kind of love that fuels religious wars and sizzles in the brainpans of madmen. Ben might have wanted to leap through a window and flee to a fortress of apathy, but this love, this intruding love, raged within his being and utterly overwhelmed all other thought, all other feeling, all other desire for action. In the moment, under the weight of love, he might have even hated Forever. It was impossible to tell.

The shifting Forever-thing stood astride the Forever-doll. Ben watched as the pieces of flesh that he'd fastidiously sewn, stitched, stapled, and glued into the doll burst from their moorings and converged on the Forever-thing, somehow melding with its bulk and congealing into a singular substance, like disparate puddles of mercury rolling together to form an uncanny lake.

The doll's head smacked against the floor, lifeless as it was intended.

The Forever-thing ambled over the dead doll and stood beside Ben. He turned his head in its direction and witnessed the end of reason. This was his Forever—a teeming mass of undifferentiated body parts, of myriad faces and torsos, hips and thighs, skins and hair, all swirling and bubbling, scattering and converging like a human kaleidoscope.

More fiery wind blew into Ben's ears.

"It is time," the collective voice whispered. "Let us . . . consummate."

Ben tried to speak, tried to ask "Why me?" or "Why us?" but could only babble incoherently. He realized the answers didn't matter, anyway. If it hadn't been him, it would have been another lonely, awkward child. The story would have played the same, with slightly different characters. It always did.

Forever knelt on the floor and placed two manically twisting, serpentine appendages on his shoulders. They burrowed under his shirt and coiled around his torso once, twice, three times, tying themselves tighter with each circumnavigation. Then they began to squeeze.

Ribs and spine, mind and spirit: all snapped and cracked under the slithering force of Forever. Ben felt its arms crushing his willpower, his identity. Memories broke off and fell to the ground; thoughts shriveled and crumbled to dust.

And, still, he couldn't bring himself to be particularly concerned. Though he should have shrieked from the agony of his skeleton's collapse or the horror of his soul's implosion, Ben could do little more than swallow a hysterical laugh. His self was melting away, disintegrating into the whirl of splintered entities within Forever, and all he could feel was love—excruciating, incommensurable, terrible love.

His relationship with Forever was finally, spectacularly, ending.

His relationship with Forever was just now beginning.

A Nuzzle, Inverted

Heavy rain melted the world beyond Brian's window, reducing hurried pedestrians to an endless stream of drab, earth-toned blobs. Brian sighed and stared at the edges of the frame, hoping to catch a glimpse of something real, something solid. There would be no living today, no meticulous construction of daily schedules and familial routines, no ascription of desires and joys, worries and terrors. Brian was hemmed into his parched pocket of existence, his basement desert where loneliness and anxiety whipped across beige-carpeted dunes. Most days, he stood on tiptoes inside the cinder-blocked cube and gazed through the tiny window that looked out onto civilization. As passersby shot past the glass, he scribbled their preciously banal stories on the walls of his skull. From morning until nightfall, he stood under the pane, imagining what it must feel like to be able to brush against other people and not break out in a cold sweat; he conceived of casual conversations in which neither speaker dug his fingernails into his palms until blood welled up beneath their blunt edges; he squeezed fleeting images of skinny jeans, flowing skirts, and shoes of all shapes and sizes into his mind, then expanded them until he had an inflated universe with which he could actually interact. Today, though, due to the downpour, there would be no big bang rushing through his brainpan. Today would be a void day.

Brian shook his head, plodded to his bathroom, and stared into the mirrored door of his medicine cabinet. A flabby, limpid ghost greeted his eyes. This was not Brian Searle. This was merely the pale remnant of a nameless boy who once dreamed he might be normal when he had finally grown into a man. But dreams never came true—not even while dreaming—and the fanged chemicals in Brian's brain had never lost their ability to strike. For the past fifteen years, he'd swilled innumerable psycho-pharmaceutical cocktails in an effort to drown out himself and replace whatever "he" was with a cardboard cutout that could at least smile at random strangers and use public toilets. No combination of drugs had ever managed to do the trick, though, and the social sphere—a plaything to most but a tauntingly precious jewel to Brian—had continued to roll further from his sweat-slicked hands. Now, at thirty-one, Brian truly felt as though his existence would always be limited to himself, a clean but ill-lit room, and the chain-rattling phantom of emptiness.

He grabbed a pair of dull scissors that were lying on the sink and plopped onto the nearby toilet seat. He stared at his bare arms, scarred and scratched as they were. Opening the scissors wide, he pressed one of the blades against his wrist. Its edge was cool, solid, and understanding. No misapprehended social cues here, no awkward silences or stumbling greetings. Pressing harder until he felt pain, Brian wondered why he never sharpened the blades.

As Brian floated in his bubble of liminal suicide, a soft scratching noise began to diffuse throughout the room. At first, he didn't hear it, utterly insulated by his funereal introspection and the ambient patter of rain against the window. However, over a matter of seconds the noise grew louder and more insistent, wiling its way into his secluded psyche and bursting any sanguinary intentions he may have held. He blinked rapidly, as if waking from a trance, dropped the scissors to the floor, and fled from the bathroom, vaguely and inexplicably panicked.

The scratching continued, louder and faster, as though something was peeling away layers of reality, tearing into Brian's apartment from an unseen dimension of space-time.

Brian paced the borders of the basement until he determined the source of the sound. It was coming from his front door—a frightening thing he only cracked open once a week, when his groceries were delivered to his below-ground stoop.

Brian stood behind the door and waited, knots balling and colliding in his stomach. The scratching did not cease. Apparently, the world beyond wanted inside.

"Hello?" Brian whispered, more to himself than to anyone or anything on the opposite side of the door.

The response: more scraping, more scratching.

"Hello?" Brian asked again, this time with enough volume so that anyone who might be nearby could hear.

Still, only scraping and scratching answered.

Wringing his quivering hands, Brian touched the doorknob and recoiled. He couldn't do this. He couldn't open the door on a non-delivery day.

The scratching continued.

Brian breathed deep. He mashed his teeth together, set his jaw, and flipped back the deadbolt. Swallowing what felt like a cannonball, he reached for the doorknob and, in one swift motion, spun it and yanked the door inward, letting the external world spill into his enclave. Instantly, rain splattered on carpet, car horns and muddled shouts rocketed along the ceiling, and the odor of a million bodies and a million engines stung Brian's nostrils.

Beneath it all, however, on the unyielding concrete doorstep, in the same place Brian's box of groceries rested every Wednesday, cowered a small, black, short-haired dog with a stunted muzzle—perhaps a strange brew of three parts Miniature Pinscher and one part pug. Its fur was matted and soaked and, even from a distance, Brian could tell that its back was covered with accumulated grime and garbage.

The dog stared up, its brown, buggy eyes gleaming. Though its tail was tucked firmly under its body, the dog reached forward with one paw, as if commanded to politely shake hands in the face of fear. Brian knelt—too quickly for a stranger—and the dog backed away, re-signing itself to the full force of the storm. As the tiny animal retreated, Brian felt a tug somewhere deep under his flesh. Though he'd never owned a dog or considered himself much of an "animal person," something drew him close to this dark little orphan. A kinship beyond reason or understanding united the two.

"Here," Brian called. "Here. I won't hurt you."

Brian remained kneeling, hands and arms out-stretched. The dog shivered and held its ground against the bottom-most step to the apartment. Minutes washed away with the draining rain. Ten. Twenty. Thirty. Brian didn't care that he was outside for so long. He didn't care that umbrella-toting pedestrians shot vaguely disapproving stares at him as they clomped along the street. The only thing that mattered was helping the dog. So, Brian waited. Outside. In full view of the omnipresent eye of People.

Finally, after what had been nearly forty-five minutes, the dog crept closer and, again, held one of its paws aloft.

Slowly, carefully, Brian slipped his hand beneath the paw; he felt its cracked pads on his palm, its pavement-hardened contours against his clammy skin. He let the dog gradually inch into his arms and, once it had acclimated itself to his scent and his threat level, he scooped it up and brought it inside, shutting the door behind him.

Hurrying to the bathroom, Brian wrapped the dog in a thick, puffy towel and rubbed it until the squirming animal no longer dripped water in its wake.

Crouched on the bathroom tile and soaked to the core, Brian stripped off his clothes and slid into a sitting position to watch the dog. Now swaddled in a warm towel and relatively dry safety, it closed its eyes and nestled on the floor. Brian laid down and curled up around it, sheltering it from the screeching, clawing everything that lurked outside. In this primal arrangement the man and the dog both fell into peaceful, unhaunted sleep—the first either one had experienced in years.

Brian woke with a series of damp squishes leaking into his ears and a musky, fecund odor coating his nostrils. Something warm and wet ran along his cheek. He opened his eyes, expecting to see the dog standing over him, licking his face. Instead, he saw a morphological monstrosity.

The creature before him—an aggregation of glistening, pulsing organs, exposed bone, and striated muscles—cocked its head to the side as it recognized that Brian had shrugged off his slumber.

Brian froze, his breath caught in his throat. Freed from their sockets, two brown, dangling eyes defied gravity and floated upward to fix him in their sight. The thing didn't attack; it just watched, still and silent.

Allowing himself to breath again, Brian surveyed the monster. It was roughly dog-shaped, but it could be no dog. In fact, Brian didn't understand how it could even be alive. With its organs out in the open, subject to the elements and the puncturing dangers of the external world, the thing had to have amazing resilience in order to survive. Brian stared at the floating eyes and the eyes, deep and old as a lost messiah's soul, stared back. He wondered if the creature was dangerous. He wondered if he was hallucinating.

Breaking eye contact, Brian glanced around the room. The tiny, frightened dog was nowhere to be found. He hoped the monster hadn't eaten it—or worse. The protruding bits of bone beneath the thing's eyes were jagged and pointy, certainly capable of shredding flesh and fur.

Suddenly, the slick, slimy creature advanced. Its muscles bunched and lengthened as it came toward Brian's mouth. Its organs throbbed with feverish desire. Viscous fluids glazed its every movement. The thing gurgled—a guttural, needful sound—and a wavering pink appendage loosened itself from the mounds of viscera. Brian screamed, lifted himself off the floor, and ran from the room, heart hammering. He flung himself behind his couch and waited, hands balled into fists.

The monster didn't give chase.

Instead, a long, wet, ripping sound slushed out of the bathroom. Brian bit the inside of his cheek to prevent himself from screaming again and peeked over the edge of the couch, into the open bathroom. The creature was missing. He let a tense minute pass then checked again. No pulsing beast. No abject horror.

Brian swiveled around the back of the couch, fists still at the ready, and crept toward the bathroom doorway. The puffy towel and Brian's crumpled clothes were spread across the floor, as before. A few smudges of dark liquid—possibly blood—dotted the towel.

Brian stopped and peeked around the corners just inside the room's entrance. Nothing waited to pounce from either spot. Cautiously, he walked in and nudged the towel with his bare foot. Nothing sprung from beneath it; nothing within its folds growled. He bent over to pick it up and examine the stains. As his line of vision lowered, he noticed a tiny, pitch-black silhouette nearly hidden within the shadows under his sink.

A wide smile exploded across his face.

"It's okay," he cooed. "It's okay, buddy. Come on out. The monster's gone. Come here. Come here."

The dog didn't budge from its hiding place.

"I bet you're hungry and thirsty," Brian said, standing upright. "Let me get you something."

He rushed to the kitchen, filled a bowl with water, and snatched a pack of turkey luncheon meat from the refrigerator. Returning to the bathroom, he tore open the pack of meat and set it, along with the bowl of water, by his feet.

With tentative steps, the dog emerged from the shadows, head held high, sniffing out molecules of sustenance. It approached the food and drink and lapped at the water, eyes never leaving Brian's towering form.

As Brian watched the dog gobble up turkey and slurp water, his thoughts returned to the monster. How had it gotten into his home? Where did it come from? Where did it go? And, most importantly, what was it?

The creature had frightened him not so much because it had done anything particularly menacing, but because it existed in such an inverted state. It seemed to have no physical defense against the stings and slings that life might throw in its path. Yet, somehow, it seemed powerful, imbued with a nameless essence that made its very being unfathomable and untouchable.

Brian shook off his contemplation and focused on the dog, which had finished its meal. He crouched, reached out, and let the dog inch into his waiting fingers.

After a few minutes of petting, he lifted the dog off its feet and carried it to the couch. He caught a glimpse of the dog's undercarriage and, if biology still held true—which, given the events of the day, might be foolhardy to believe—his newfound friend was male.

"A boy," Brian said, stroking the dog's head as it sat

beside him on the couch, "what's a good name for a boy?"

The dog cocked his head to one side, apparently invested in Brian's decision.

"How about . . . Doug?" Brian asked. "That's 'dog' with a 'u' in it."

The dog moved forward and nuzzled under Brian's hand.

"Doug it is! Doug Dog!" he laughed.

Brian turned on the TV and Doug cuddled beside him. It took all of Brian's willpower to restrain himself from raising the tiny animal to his chest and hugging it until the two melded.

"Doug, Doug, Doug," Brian repeated quietly, a mantra for all the unexpected rainbows that might miraculously burst through the otherwise oppressive maelstrom of daily living.

Sometimes the things that save you are the things that need the most saving themselves, Brian thought, flashes of scissors against wrists streaking across his cortex.

Doug pressed himself tight against Brian's thigh.

"Doug, Doug, Doug," he whispered in response.

A few hours later, while Brian watched a late-night comedy show, Doug's intestines began to rumble and shake, as though a seismic shift was occurring deep beneath the continent of his body. The dog made no overtures toward the door, so Brian doubted he had to relieve his bowels or bladder. He stroked Doug's back, thinking that the upheaval could be no more than indigestion.

Generally unconcerned, he flipped a channel and dove back into the digital sea.

But the rumbling grew worse.

Doug's entire body vibrated with some sort of internal energy. He opened his mouth wide—a gesture that seemed sure to indicate a puddle of vomit was on the horizon—and let loose a few strange crackles, sounds that echoed the clattering of bones and the twisting of ligaments and tendons.

At the sound, Brian dove off the couch and knelt in front of Doug, still rubbing the dog's back.

"Doug? Doug? What's wrong, buddy?" Brian asked, panic stabbing every syllable. "What's wrong? Do you need to go outside? Doug?"

Doug's mouth remained open and, if it was possible, seemed to unhinge, such that his lower jaw stretched until it was perpendicular to its brother above. And it didn't stop. The dog's mouth broke even wider, pushing backward against its torso, while its upper parts flew in an arc in the opposite direction. Doug's head was, impossibly, turning inside-out.

"Oh shit. Oh shit. Shit, shit, shit. What do I do? What do I do? Don't die. Please don't die," Brian moaned.

Doug raised a paw, as he'd done on the stoop what seemed like lifetimes ago.

While Brian's shaking hand met and engulfed the vibrating paw, his eyes skittered around the apartment, seeking help. On the counter in his kitchen, Brian spied his cell phone. He ran to it, flipped it open and punched in a number, then returned to Doug's side with 9-1-1 glowing bright on the its display.

In the brief moment he was gone, Doug's entire face

had become the visage of roadkill, a hunk of fibrous muscle and rolled away tissue that left jagged, ragged exposed bone. Truth fell from the sky and crushed Brian's mind.

He dropped his phone and watched, awestruck, as the transformation rippled from nose to tail. Doug's entire body was turning itself inside-out, his innermost being—a complex system of tender parts and hidden interactions—revealing itself to Brian's concerned gaze.

As the fleshy shell opened onto a series of glistening crimson and purple pearls, Brian found his hand reaching out to touch Doug's new form. The dog-creature didn't back away or flee; rather, he leaned into Brian's light touch.

Brian stroked Doug and Doug—the real, unmasked Doug—moved forward, a pink appendage snaking out from the rest of his beautifully convoluted mass. Brian let it flick up and down his fingers and his wrist, no longer terrified of its implications. It was, after all, just the dislocated tongue of a loving canine companion.

Sliding his hand back and forth over Doug's back, Brian began to see marks scouring the muscle and organs. Whitish streaks cut across most—if not all—of the dog's innards. Brian leaned in closer and realized he was witnessing the end-product of physical trauma. Beaten, kicked, slapped, or punched, Doug had been abused.

Tears welled up at the edges of his eyelids. He hadn't cried since he was a child, but this evidence of abuse caused his walls to erode.

"Why?" he whispered. "Why would someone do that to you?"

Inverted Doug simply pressed closer.

Brian realized the answer was, of course, under his hand.

Someone who had pledged responsibility and care for Doug—maybe many such people—had seen this inverse side, this heap of sanguine fibers and pustules, and believed it to be, as Brian first had, a hideous affront to nature. At first, before they knew, these people would have given Doug food, shelter, and maybe even love. And Doug, for his part, would have given love back and allowed himself the tentative freedom to be the being he truly was—a bizarre, tangled mess of a dog. But the people didn't like what they saw when Doug revealed himself; they turned away in disgust, probably fear. Some undoubtedly ran. Some chased Doug outside and locked the door behind him. Others hit Doug until he shifted back, into a form that they could understand, a form in which they could easily find their preconceptions and beliefs, a form that, in some haphazard way, mirrored their own. Doug's life must have been hell. Never to be able to vomit himself forth, to make any connection with the people and things outside himself: this was Doug's curse. He was a monster.

But he was also a very good dog.

Tears cascaded from Brian's cheeks. He understood so well. He pulled Doug tight to his chest and petted the dog's beating heart, glancing up to the window that was still streaked by rain. He understood oh so very well.

Suddenly, a balmy, tingling sensation passed over Brian. He felt as Atlas might if the world upon his shoulders suddenly crumbled to dust. Without worry, without shame, without fear of reprisal, Brian laughed, still crying, and, into Doug's shorn face, breathed "Doug

Doug Doug. You're a good boy, Doug. You're a good boy."

He stroked the inverted dog's head and noticed the skin on his finger beginning to unzip, flesh and fatty lumps rolling back, back into a place where they had no purpose or meaning. Along his outer thighs, he could already feel his muscle peeling away, marrow deep within his bones reaching out to the surface. The process wasn't pain; it was relief. It was escape.

Brian moved onto the couch and let Doug slide into his lap. Fingers now little more than gristly clumps, he rubbed behind his dog's ears.

One of Brian's eyes popped free of its socket and Doug's serpentine tongue shot up to lick it.

Brian chuckled.

They would be monsters together, then, and that was all Brian could have ever hoped for.

Crowning

They called the disease epidermal fertilosis.
Some said it was a plague.

Others claimed it was a miracle.

In either case, the woman on the opposite side of the waiting room had contracted it in a very bad way.

Five massive tumescent sacs covered her body, the most noticeable an inflamed bulb that ran from the base of her jaw to the top of her shoulder and caused her head to tilt at a precarious angle.

The sac pulsed.

I slouched deeper into my chair.

The woman flashed a wide smile at me, half her teeth broken or missing.

"Twins. They're always kickin'," she laughed.

The sac pulsed again, harder, and began to strain away from the woman's neck. Her eyes bulged. Her skin flushed. She stood, as though to signal for help, but, instead, made a wet, gurgling sound and collapsed to the floor. Her entire body twisted and writhed as sacs on her stomach, back, and legs also tried to break free from their moorings, perhaps sensing imminent danger.

A nurse breezed into the waiting room from some unseen deathbed, glanced at the twitching woman on the floor, and blew away as quickly and mysteriously as he'd entered.

I remained frozen.

The woman on the floor squirmed toward me, still smiling.

With trembling hand, she pointed to the neck-sac.

"Help. My babies," she choked, and fell back against the concrete floor, neck-sac bursting upon impact.

I couldn't help but watch in wonder as strange liquids streamed out from a million perforations in the heavily striated flesh. My stomach groaned. My bowels clenched. Life oozed from the sac—deep red, yellow-green, off-white, black and brown all mixing together, pouring forth in rivulets of undifferentiated potential.

Suddenly, from out of the pools of muck and gore, a tiny hand reared up. It clawed through the open wound and yanked at loose flaps of torn skin, seeking purchase into the world beyond the woman's neck. I felt compelled to help. I felt compelled to kill.

I did neither.

The other sacs continued to struggle for freedom, pulsing and straining outward in an attempt to escape their prisons of dying tissue. But none burst open. None tore through, save that one wavering, grasping hand.

I bent low in my chair and glanced at the woman's face. Though the tensile strength of her muscles had expired, her smile, inexplicably, remained.

The hand and its five tiny fingers continued to slash

through the antiseptic air.
    I shrugged and shivered.
    The nurse did not return.

Rub-A-Dub-Dub

They were three men adrift on an ocean of remorse—or, at least, they were supposed to be.

Henry Hickson, a butcher.

Anthony Castro, a baker.

And LeMont Curry, an artisan candle maker.

Three criminals.

Three sacrificial lambs.

In their tiny, rusted, auto-piloting barge—a "Tub," as was its idiomatic term among survivors—they floated ever onward, closer to Thalak, the Old One, the Scourge, the immense, psychic, pulsing thing in the sea that had so far killed or driven mad roughly half the earth's population. When the trio reached Thalak's edge, they would be engulfed within its maroon folds, swallowed whole, and digested so that the god could continue its reign of slow decay. They would provide sustenance for the great, miserable thing and—in death, in punishment—aid in its apocalypse.

But, for the moment, they were alive. And they were

anxious, albeit for very different reasons.

Hickson kicked against his shackles—bolted tight to the tub's iron deck—and swore.

"We can't just sit here until the end," he growled. "There's gotta be a way to break free."

Castro, eyes closed and lying prone under the blazing noonday sun, sighed and shook his head. Under his breath, barely a whisper to the other two, he muttered "It was trying to get free that landed us here."

Hickson ignored him and, again, strained against the shackles. He was rewarded with only pain, a trickle of blood, and frustration.

He shook his sweat-laden head and slumped to the deck. "These are the only damn things that still work in this world."

Balled up in a thin strip of shade opposite Hickson, Curry stared at the butcher's struggle. A grin rose at one corner of his mouth. "What would you do if you could break them?"

Hickson glanced up and scowled. "You think this is funny? You think sitting here on death's cruise ship is fun?"

Amusement still fixed upon his lips, Curry shook his head. "Not in the slightest. I just wondered if you had a plan. If, you know, you actually snapped through them."

Hickson glared at the candle maker, then broke off his gaze and looked to the preternaturally placid waters surrounding them.

"Actually, I do," he said, his words falling solid, determined, resigned to an endless war.

"Really? And what's that?" Curry asked, sitting upright and unfurling his thin, spindly legs.

Hickson shifted and reached into his waistband at the small of his back. He withdrew from its confines a narrow, sheathed cleaver. Holding it up before his face, he slipped off its leather case and let daylight glint against tempered steel.

"This," he said. "This is my plan."

Castro rolled onto his side and squinted at the blade.

"That's your object of remembrance?" he asked, a tremolo of trepidation creeping into the question. "What did you do?"

Curry cocked his head to the side and squinted at the shining blade. "Good question. And, more to the point, what exactly are you going to do with that?" He motioned to the cleaver.

Hickson remained silent, studying his tool. What he saw upon its surface—his reflection or his sins or maybe even a past foolishly cut through with hope—Curry and Castro could not know.

Finally, after what seemed like hours, Hickson began to speak, a low, brooding volcano within this throat erupting vengeance and sorrow.

"What I'm going to do with this," he said, slashing the cleaver through the air, "is find a justice that's been missing for a very long time, a justice that my wife and my daughter deserve."

Castro shook his head and again rolled onto his back.

"There is no justice in this world," he said. "No justice at all. Just legitimized prejudice and revenge."

"Fine," Hickson rumbled. "Fine. Justice, revenge, prejudice—whatever you want to call it, I'm going to have it. That monstrosity in the sea deserves every swing of my arm and every letter of my family's name I'm going to carve into it."

Curry slid forward, somehow still in shadow, and asked, eyes slivered, "And why is that? What's brought you to this tub? What did Thalak do to you other than destroying life as we all knew it? What makes *your* crusade so important?"

Hickson rubbed his eyes and, under stricture of the shackles, stood as best he could.

"Back on land," he said, turned toward the glass ocean, perhaps seeking the memory of a man he'd once been, "I was a butcher. Before the purges, before the concentration zones, I ran a little shop in a little town in a part of Pennsylvania that most people would only visit if they were lost or on a hunting trip. My wife, Val, worked part-time at Wal-Mart during the day, but she helped out at night, wrapping, packing, feeding the grinder if someone wanted ground meat. It was a twenty-four hour affair during deer season. Pretty successful, all in all. We made a decent living. Owned a little ranch-style house. Sometimes we hiked the mountains on weekends. Sometimes we rode four-wheelers—you know, ATVs—over our neighbors' unkempt fields for fun. Did a lot of target shooting and beer drinking at our friends' places. You could've called us hicks, I guess. I just thought of us as rugged.

"We had a daughter, too. Black hair, green eyes. Like a cat. Kitty, we called her, though her name was actually Stephanie. Smart. Too smart. She knew when and how to bend the truth so that she'd get her own way. She probably would've made a good lawyer in another place and time. She was everything for me and Val. She was our first, our only. And she was barely four when Thalak rose, when it hit us all with that very first psycho purge.

"Val didn't survive it. Happened a Sunday afternoon, you remember that? I was outside, doing something that now seems like a stupid waste of time—planting new bushes or weed whacking or something like that. I remember smelling grass, then this . . . weight. This unbelievable squeezing weight. You know what I mean. Thalak's feelers. I knew that something big and powerful and beyond my sense of . . . of . . . well, everything, was searching me over, hard, and boring into my thoughts. And that's when I heard Kitty screaming. She and Val had been baking cookies for her to take to her preschool class. Val's eyes had burst right in front of her. There was blood dripping from my daughter's lips. Four years old. Her face covered with her mother's ruined brain. Apparently Thalak saw something in Val's head it didn't like, some kind of rebellion that I didn't have in me and Kitty couldn't yet understand.

"After that, for a long time, Kitty was never more than ten feet from me. I had only to look over my shoulder and there she'd be, standing behind me, waiting for me to tell her that everything would be okay or that the people she saw wandering the roads—the strange, hairless, overly-tanned men and women in dark red clothes—didn't mean anything. Of course, I couldn't tell her that. All I could do was hug her. And even that didn't help much, because soon the strange men and women, the bishops, came with their disciples and rounded us up. They took us to the Baltimore CZ, which is where I guess you guys ended up, too, since we're all on this tub together.

"In the Balt CZ, for the past eight years, I continued to butcher what few livestock they let us have. I bought chickens and pigs when I could and tried to run a small shop again. Mostly, it was a failure. Whenever I actually had meat on the shelves, the bishops would stop in and take all of it for their ceremonies and feasts. Never paid me a dime. 'Communal tithing,' they called it. The price to be protected from Thalak by its own servants. Bullshit. Communal tithing left us without electricity half the year and without food some weeks.

"Kitty—now 'Cat,' as she insisted being called after she turned ten—had no interest in butchery. She started going out, getting away from me and our rundown shack. She spent a lot of time at the tiny CZ library, reading books about spies and heists and back alley deals. Crime drama stuff. She said she wanted to be master thief. I laughed and thought 'whatever.' Just a kid's hope to have more than four walls and a bed, which, really, was about all we did have back there. But Cat didn't cause trouble in the education center and she didn't have 'bad' friends, so I wasn't worried about her. I was more worried about where our next meal would come from. After all, we couldn't live on water and old jerky year-round.

"Somehow we always scraped by. A tough life, not many frills, but okay, considering half the world was dead and even more of it was dying. One thing I always made sure of, though, regardless of how hungry I was or how much the roof leaked or how long I chopped and hacked in the shop: on Cat's birthday, I bought her something nice. One year, a huge stuffed dog. Another year, a crystal statue of a dragon—she loved dragons for some reason. Last year, a gold locket with Val's picture inside. I tried . . . I tried to make sure she felt that surviving this hell another year was something to celebrate. I tried to make her feel special, even if that word doesn't mean anything anymore.

"Well, this year, being twelve and ready to take on the world, Cat apparently decided that for my birthday—a big one, I turned forty—*she* needed to get something impressive for *me*. But she had no money. No allowance, obviously. Nothing but her mind. Her sharp, beautiful mind. And so she did what she wanted to all along: she became a thief. She went out one night, broke into a general goods store, and stole a set of Shun Pro Sho knives. They were behind thick glass, in a case with jewelry and guns and other stuff that no one can afford now. She picked them because they looked, she said, 'like the knives of an ancient warrior.'

"When I unwrapped them on my birthday, I knew it wasn't right. These were expensive pieces of cutlery. Really expensive. Even before Thalak took over, a set of these things would've cost four hundred or five hundred dollars. I didn't know how Cat had gotten them. I couldn't know. But I figured it couldn't be legit. So I just smiled and hugged her and hid my shaking hands in my pockets. They were the best birthday present I'd ever gotten. They were also the worst.

"Two days later, the bishops came to our house. They knew. They always knew. Thalak is constantly watching. It wasn't a matter of proving guilt or innocence. It was a matter of deciding the severity of her punishment.

"The bishops held one of their trials. I spoke for my daughter. I showed them her record at the education center. I explained that without her mother, she had a hole in her life. I said she was just a kid and kids make mistakes and that she wasn't trying to hurt anyone. They didn't care. They asked Cat why she did it, why she stole knives that were worth more than her father's entire business. She answered 'Because my dad deserves to have something more than just me.' "

"The bishops didn't think so. They're nothing if not thorough. They had researched her library checkouts and knew she'd been reading about crime for the past couple years. They knew her interests and her strengths. They knew she would only get better at stealing as she grew older. At only twelve, she'd found her way into a closed shop and into a secure case without setting off any alarms. The bishops were worried about the future, worried that Cat would end up stealing bigger things, more important things, secret, powerful things that no one should ever own. And so they sentenced her to the Tub. Twelve years old. Sentenced to be sacrificed.

"Their official reason—I memorized it—was that 'as theft is indicative of rebellion against the accepted social framework, the girl poses a long-term risk to the stability of the Order of Thalak, as she may incite or perpetrate more significant acts of disruption as she ages.' I threw curses at the judge who read that decision. I leaped out of my chair and rushed him and punched him, square between those glassy blue eyes that all the bishops have."

"They gave me six months in prison for that punch. I sat in a concrete cell and refused to eat or drink, but the bishops strapped me to a table and injected me with fluids to keep me alive. Six months. I never saw Cat chained to the deck of a tub. I never had the chance to hug her or kiss her one last time. I never waved to her as the tub drifted off to Thalak. I never got the opportunity to say to my daughter 'whatever else happens, I'm proud of you.' No. I was in a concrete block. For six months. And then, I was released. And my life was supposed to go on.

"But the sun didn't shine as bright anymore and the air didn't smell as crisp. Our house—now just my house—didn't feel like a house anymore. It was the waiting room to death. My wife, gone. My daughter, gone. My livelihood, gone. Even the knives were gone; the entire set was sent off with Cat as her object of remembrance.

"For a while, I tried to continue living. I tried to go about my daily business. But all I could see was flames and all I could hear were the terrified pleas of bishops as I kicked in their leathery faces. I wasted into a pit of hatred. And that's when I realized what I had to do. I had to stand up and take back my world. And the only way to do it was to destroy the things that had taken my world from me: Thalak and its Order.

"So I planned. I used every last cent I had to buy four fat hogs and twenty chickens—more than I'd ever had in Baltimore. I prepared them and stuck them in the front window of my dilapidated shop. I knew the bishops would come for them. They always did. And I wasn't disappointed.

"The very same day I put the meat out for display, three bishops stopped in and claimed they needed a tithe. They wanted my entire stock for a rising celebration. I was ready. I told them that I had even more in back; I told them they should come with me and I'd show them. I led them past the prep tables to the killing floor. Three bishops. They didn't expect it. Few people are crazy enough to attack bishops, knowing what will happen if they do. But I didn't care. I just wanted to feel a sense of purpose again, like something I did actually had meaning, like my cleaver might be able to speak the same language that Thalak spoke. And it did. Every swipe and every cut gave Cat words that the bishops would understand. Every spray of blood gave Val a chance to defend her thoughts in the court of Thalak.

"When it was over, the killing floor was a mess. I didn't feel sorry for what I'd done. I didn't really believe that the bishops were people any more; they'd given up their humanity when they accepted a permanent connection to Thalak. No, I didn't feel sorry at all. I felt relieved. I felt that Cat and Val had to be more at peace now. A very small justice had been done.

"That night, a dozen bishops came for me. Big, strong, muscled bishops. I killed two. Clean slices across their throats. But the rest piled on me and knocked me out.

"They sentenced me to the Tub. Obviously there was no other option. But that's fine by me, because now I can go to Thalak, I can go to death, with my fists tight and my blades swinging. I know I can't beat a god, but maybe I can scar it just a little. Maybe I can make it feel, for a split second, the same kind of pain it inflicts on us every day. That's my crusade. That's my justice. That's all I have left and that's all I—as nothing more than a stupid, simple man—can do."

Hickson nodded to himself and closed his eyes. The immutable thrum of the barge's motor underscored his conclusion.

Curry applauded, each smack of his hands rocketing across the too-bright sky.

"Good show, Mr. Butcher. Good show. I like you," he said, a hard speckle of admiration in his tone. "You have potential."

Castro groaned and sat upright.

"You have to be kidding me," he said. "You can't possibly believe your daughter would have been better off living. Her sentence was a mercy. Dying was the best possible future for her."

Hickson's eyelids flew open. He lunged toward Castro but his shackles tripped him before he could reach the baker. He tumbled to the rusty deck, still gripping his cleaver tight.

A wheezy, deflated laugh slipped from Castro's chapped lips.

"She was the only good and decent thing in this world," Hickson said, picking himself up off the deck. "You aren't either of those things."

Castro shook his head and laughed again, mirthless.

"You don't know me," he said "And you really don't know what 'good' or 'decent' is. Let me tell you: 'good' and 'decent' don't apply to the living any more. We're all damned. We're all in hell. And Thalak is the devil. 'Good' is getting out of this place and 'decent' is having the willpower to do it. So your daughter dying? Yes, that's 'good.' "

Hickson tensed as though to lunge at Castro again. His grasp on his cleaver closed ever harder and his knuckles popped white and huge against the strain.

"Gentlemen," Curry said, spreading his arms in entreaty but refusing to move from his shade, "let's not turn on each other. We have a common enemy and we're going to meet it in all its putrescent glory in a few very short hours. We should remember too keep our priorities in order."

Hickson considered for a moment then slumped to the deck.

"So just who are you, then?" he asked Castro. "You, who knows so much about good and evil?"

"No one," the baker answered. "No one important."

A weak, fetid breeze lazed over the tub.

Castro reached into one of his pants pockets and pulled forth a chunk of bread.

"This, though," he said, raising the bread above his head reverentially, "this *is* important. This is righteousness, and I am its slave."

Hickson grunted and turned away.

"So you're insane. Great."

Curry slid closer to the baker and the butcher and, again, the shadows in which he reclined seemed to stretch with his movement. His coal-flecked eyes glittered in the darkness.

"He might be insane," Curry said, "but I doubt it. He has a reason for what he does. Isn't that right, Gravebaker?"

Hickson shot a worried glance at Curry.

"Gravebaker?" he mouthed.

Curry nodded.

Castro held the bread to his heart and scowled.

"I hate that name. It sounds entirely . . . grotesque. The people who coined it don't understand."

"Understand what, precisely?" Curry asked.

Castro laid back and spread his arms and legs wide. Splayed on the deck, an asterisk in the grand narrative of existence, he shouted at the sky.

"They don't understand that I've never intended to harm anyone . . . at least, not in the long-term. I don't laugh like a hackneyed villain as those I help buy their daily bread and I don't dance gleefully in the silhouette of their trespasses. I'm not a demon or a hobgoblin or a monster in the mist. No, no, no. I'm only . . . I'm only someone who's prematurely reached the conclusion that we all must reach one day."

"And that conclusion is?" Curry's prompt hissed out of the umbra in which he slouched.

Another tide of putrefied fish and stagnant water rolled over the air.

"Life is too much effort to live," the baker said. "At some point everyone releases, everyone allows all physical bindings to fall away. Maybe by coercion, maybe by necessity, maybe by sheer desperate hopefulness of something else beyond. One way or the other, we all do it eventually. We all let go. We all *must* let go.

"That wasn't an easy truth for me to find. I grew up in a house so thick with Christ that you could taste the salt of his hallowed sweat as he hung on his cross. In every room, a crucifix. My parents and my uncles and my aunts and my cousins and my friends—everyone I knew called themselves 'Catholic.' For years, I didn't know what that meant because I had nothing to compare it to. My family lived in Miami in a mostly isolated Puerto Rican community where it felt like everyone called themselves 'Catholic' whether they believed in God or not. I went to a school where all the teachers were either my 'father' or 'mother' or 'sister,' even though they weren't related to me. I prayed to a corpse who was supposed to be powerful, even though it didn't have clothes and apparently couldn't beat anyone in a fistfight. I revealed all my sins and secrets to a man in a dark room, even though I wasn't supposed to talk to strange men. And I called myself 'Catholic,' too, even though I had no real idea what it meant.

"Well, when I was eleven, I realized what it meant—to me, at least. That year, my father, a chubby, soft-spoken man who forever smelled of acrid mass production, was accidentally shot and killed during a mugging. He'd been walking home from the bus stop after finishing a late shift at the plastics factory where he worked. He had fifty-nine dollars on him.

"The night my father was murdered, I watched my mother, a tiny woman who wore huge silver crosses in her ears and around her neck, take off her jewelry and squeeze it in her hands until blood streamed down her arms. She told me that God had a plan for taking my father, though we couldn't know it, and that it was our part in the world to endure the pain of His wisdom.

"And so I did. I let the pain flood through me. At my little league games, I forced myself to stare at the empty spot between my mother and my sister. During dinner, I passed plates of empanadas and tostones toward the vacant chair at the head of our dining room table. When I loaded up video games that my father and I used to play together, I'd make sure to sign in a second player and let it sit, idle, frozen in place and barring my own progress. Kneeling beside my bed before I went to sleep, I'd ask the Lord to inflict pain upon me, to heap it upon my soul, if that would mean my father had a meaningful place, a grander purpose, in His kingdom.

"I understood then. Faith by any name and any form meant suffering for a purpose.

"As years passed, I devoted more and more of my time to my church. I ran administrative errands for the padres; I worked bake sales and fell into baking as a hobby, and later an occupation, because of my participation; I packed my bags and flew off to dusty African huts with stacks of Bibles; I built churches in Haiti, in Costa Rica, in Guatemala. And all along, I hated it. I hated missing my father when I knew I wasn't supposed to. I hated serving a master that neither thanked me nor paid me the slightest regard. Most of all, I hated my friends from school who weren't as devout as I was. They all seemed to have so much . . . fun.

"They dated and had sex and drank and smoked weed and threw parties that I was never invited to. I wanted the abandon they possessed so easily. I wanted it desperately. I discussed my problems with the priests at my church and one man in particular, Father Guillen. Father Guillen had been the priest who presided over my father's funeral. Like my father, he was gentle in tone and affable in spirit. Often, he said to me 'Remember: your friends might believe they're having a good time and you might even believe it, but they aren't going to enjoy the rewards of the spirit that you will, in the end. Let them have their parties. You're organizing one in heaven.'

"And so I persevered. I opened a bakery and donated a quarter of my profits to the church. I ate dinner with Father Guillen once a week. We conversed about the weakness of the flesh, the glory of God, the pitching staff of the Marlins, and the proper thickness of a quality ganache icing. He convinced me to remain steadfast and chaste and, when I did, I could see in his weathered smile and his droopy eyes a pride for me like maybe my own father might have had.

"For years, I baked and I prayed and I confessed and I burned with desires. But I didn't give in. I just thought of my father, perhaps at the Lord's left hand, and Father

Guillen, whose pat on the shoulder would have to suffice for a loving embrace. For all its redundant pains and defeated ambitions, life, I was convinced, held one purpose: successfully reaching the next. I was well on my way to sainthood.

"And then Thalak rose.

"When it unleashed its first psycho purge, it sought out those who would oppose it and crushed them before they had the opportunity, yes, but it also sought out those who would obey it. That first psycho purge recruited the initial body of the Order, and most of the bishops, most of the pious, came from the ranks of those who already bowed to a god.

"All those uncles and aunts and cousins who genuflected and called themselves 'Catholic' suddenly drew three-pointed figures in the air over their chests and called themselves 'Thalic.' My mother replaced the crosses in her ears and on her neck with Thalak's symbol—the triad of red triangles. Worst of all, though, Father Guillen . . . Father Guillen lost his hair. His skin turned a darker shade, an unnatural shade, overnight. And his eyes . . . lightened . . . until they became the blue of the Order.

"Christianity, Judaism, Islam, Hinduism: they weren't stomped out by the new god, as a lot of people think. They were absorbed.

"As for me, apparently Thalak knew the conflict in my soul and decided it was impediment enough to both keep me on as a slave and keep me out of the Order. Everyone else in my life, all the people who I had counted on to believe in something, to give order to the senselessness of . . . of everything . . . well, those people were suddenly wearing red and worshiping a behemoth jellyfish in the sea.

"I couldn't fathom the change. How could the faithful convert so easily, so readily? What would God do to them? What would Jesus think? How would they ever enter heaven?

"Before I was sent north, first to the Savannah CZ and then on to Baltimore, I went to see Father Guillen—now under a crimson frock—one last time. I asked him 'How could you forsake the Lord? How could you turn away from everything you held dear and follow that monster in the ocean?'

"And you know what he said to me? New eyes sparkling, he said 'I follow the one true God, Anthony. I've always followed the one true God. It's just that now God has finally revealed Itself and Its ultimate plan for the world. God is out there, ready to destroy, ready to remake the world in Its image, as foretold in scripture. God is hallowed, my son, and Thalak be Its name.'

"Even then, I still didn't understand. I didn't get it. Until . . . until they rounded us up to move to Savannah and I watched as Father Guillen beat an old neighbor woman to death because she refused to leave her house. He pounded her head against the sidewalk and smiled as he did it. And when he was finished, he tri-flected and uttered some oath to Thalak.

"That's when it all cracked apart, into place. Faith didn't mean suffering for a purpose. It just meant suffering.

"Life wasn't given to us so that we could get to heaven. Life just *was*. No meaning. No purpose. Only screaming agony coming in and screaming agony going out. People believed in something—heaven or nirvana or whatever—

so they wouldn't have to face the truth that their pains, their misfortunes, had no meaning. My friends from long ago didn't fuck and get high because they'd lost their way or were tempted by some dark force; they fucked and got high to escape the pain of existence. Everything . . . everything without objective meaning. My father died just because some asshole wanted drug money. Millions died just because some dimension-hopping creature stumbled upon Earth and wanted to play. It was all . . . excruciating nothingness.

"And so, alone in the Savannah CZ, my family and friends now sequestered away in the Order villages, I came unglued. I still baked and traded my wares in the Order's new barter economy, but when I wasn't making something in the kitchen I was passed out drunk on the floor. I cried. I laughed. I laughed and cried at the same time. I intentionally cut my arms with bread knives and told myself it was accidental. I sank into that Georgia swamp.

"But it was in the Savannah CZ that I met the ancient girl.

"Twice a week—always on Saturdays and Wednesdays —this same girl bought a loaf of rye bread at the street-corner stand where I sold my goods. She was young. Twenty-one or twenty-two, maybe. Pretty, too. But for all intents and purposes she might as well have been an old crone. Her shoulders slouched, her face never broke from an aloof frown, and when she spoke it was in blank, ghostly tones, as though she'd witnessed all the atrocities in all the wars in human history.

"I didn't think much about her, falling as I was down my own rabbit hole. But, one random Saturday, apropos of nothing, she explained why she bought bread. Standing bent at my makeshift booth, she said 'My mother and my son loved eating rye. It was their special treat. They'd slice up a fresh tomato and slather the bread with mayo, then put it all together and munch away on the back porch. They watched dragonflies out there and told stories to each other. But they were taken in the purges. I never go out on the porch anymore. I can't stand rye bread, either. But I force myself to eat it at every meal so that I remember them. So that they're not entirely lost. So that I'm not entirely lost.'

"For the ancient girl, there was no past or future. Her links to both had been severed. All she had left was the present, a constant drone of guilt and suffering and terror. She had no joy, no true hope. Only bread.

"It was there and then that I decided I was going to help humanity in its time of need. I was going to give people what they really wanted, what they really needed: release.

"I began to experiment with various poisonous chemicals and ways of getting them into or onto my baked goods. I decided the best way would be to include them in a buttery glaze brushed on after the breads or cakes had risen and cooled. I wanted fast acting, painless poisons, but mostly I could only find arsenic and arsenic derivatives. Fast acting, yes. Painless, not a chance. Even so, I accepted it. The pain I inflicted was a means to an end, and my end, the end we all must come to, the great release from all this suffering, was more important.

"So, once I had the process perfected, I sold the ancient girl a special loaf. It was a Wednesday. She never showed on Saturday. Or the next Wednesday. Or the Saturday after that. I helped her let go.

"Shortly thereafter, the bishops sent me on to Baltimore with a transfer group. And this is where you both know me from, obviously. There, I helped sixty-six more people who came to my booth. Sixty-six people who were avatars of torment. Now, they're free. They're not suffering. They're not soul-stricken. They're just . . . gone.

"I'm urban legend in the Baltimore CZ, I know, but no one should have ever feared me. Not the bishops, for being their competition, and certainly not the average man and woman on the street. I don't murder. I never did and I never will. I only release. With this most wonderful of truths . . ."

Castro held the bread beneath his nose and breathed deep. The odor of rot crouched heavy in the air.

"So he's not just insane, he thinks he's some kind of goddamned messiah, too," Hickson spat.

During Castro's story, Curry had retreated to the darkest shadows on his side of the tub. There he sat, curled like Rodin's Thinker.

"I told you, the Gravebaker isn't insane," he said. "At least, no more than anyone else still left. A famous serial killer, yes. A man with a middling philosophy, yes. But not insane."

Ignoring them both, Castro continued to cradle his bread to his face.

The tub motored onward, tugged by psychokinetic forces beyond mortal control.

Hickson set to work chopping at his shackles with the cleaver but they offered no discernible weakness. He soon abandoned the idea and, instead, began to examine his ankles, squeezing and prodding the area just above the reach of the restraints.

To either side of the tub, a series of black dots began to blink into view—other tubs, thousands of tubs, from other concentration zones around the world, all carrying trios of sacrificial criminals.

At the horizon's edge stretched a vast line of richest red, as though the space where sea and sky met had been opened like the wrist of a suicide.

"Do you see it out there?" Curry asked no one in particular. "It's waiting. It's always been waiting, somewhere. It's always known every single life it will snuff out, every action it will take, and every action that will be taken against it. It knows the exact moment and place and manner of its death. Can you imagine? Can you even dream of what it must be like to perceive time that way, as an immutable, static dimension rather than a dynamic, flowing succession? Everything for Thalak is already dead; everything will always be alive. Nothing will ever change. No wonder it wants to destroy the universe. I almost feel . . . sorry for it."

Hickson rolled his eyes and shook his head.

"So *you're* crazy, too. Great."

"How do you know so much about Thalak's mind?" Castro mumbled from beneath his bread.

Curry smiled wide. It had been years since either Hickson or Castro had seen a genuine, undefeated smile. Somehow, the gesture seemed perverse.

"I have inside information," he replied. "I know all about Thalak. And much, much more."

Hickson sighed, reclined against his side of the boat, and folded his arms over his chest.

"Alright," he said, "I'll bite. What's your deal? What do you know? Why are you on this tub?"

"Do you want the long version or short version?" Curry countered. "Short version: I'm here because I committed sacrilege. The bishops caught me communing with . . . ah . . . something not quite Thalic."

Hickson cocked an eyebrow.

"Sacrilege? How's that possible? I thought the only two religions left were fear and The Order."

"Sound like the same thing to me," Castro coughed.

For the first time since they'd been bolted to the tub, Curry rose to his feet. Inexplicably, unbelievably, the surrounding shadows rose with him. He waved a hand and they spread out from his side of the barge until they enveloped the two other men. Their touch raised goose flesh wherever they glided over uncovered skin.

Hickson dropped his cleaver, which clattered to the deck.

Castro, no longer tormented by the afternoon heat, skittered to and fro, as though a bug on a hotplate.

Wrapped in shade cast from nowhere, Hickson muttered "What the hell . . . ?" and looked up into the cloudless, sunlit sky.

"There are," Curry said, seemingly floating toward the butcher and the baker, "other possibilities."

He reached into a shirt pocket and produced a short, thin, unremarkable white candle.

"Life, as both of you have so succinctly explained, is not a course of straight lines and right angles; it's a helical infinity, curving backward, forward, into places we can never imagine.

"Myself, for example. I was orphaned when I was four. I don't remember my father at all. I suppose he was really just a fifty dollar bill in my mother's pocket. She was a heroin addict and, apparently, she prostituted to feed her demon. I don't remember her doing it, but several of my foster parents were more than happy to share that crumb of information with me when I misbehaved.

"Still, I don't remember my mother being a strung-out whore. In fact, I only have one real memory of her: she's holding a heated frying pan over my head—I don't know what's in it, probably breakfast for me—and the scalding grease from whatever she's cooking is splattering out, flying in all directions, pocking the walls with dark spots and my body with pinpricks of scalding oil. It hurts. It hurts so much. But I don't cry out. I don't move. I just sit in my chair and I wait for my mother to either spill everything in the pan onto me or feed me. Boiling death or glorious satiation—I don't know which is coming. But I do know that, one way or the other, whether my mother hurts me worse or makes me feel better, there's only one road to escape: detachment. If I flail out and try to move from under the pan, fearing burns, I might hit her arm and she might spill it due to my flurry; if I try to grab it from her and take the food, hoping to fill my rumbling stomach, I might spill it on myself. The only way to survive is to sit back and let go of hope, let go of fear. Just . . . watch, be careful, and accept whatever falls from the pan—oil or bacon, pain or delight. And so I do. I sit back and wait for whatever comes next. And you know what happens in that memory? My mother doesn't spill that sizzling greasepan. But she doesn't give me its contents, either. No. You know what she does? She heaves it through a closed window, glass shattering into a billion sparkly bits, and screams at someone outside, then launches herself through the open pane and takes chase of whoever invoked her ire.

"The future, the past: places we can never imagine.

"In any case, one day not long after that memory, my mother never returned home and the government—men in blue polo shirts who smelled of wintergreen—came and took me away. So I grew up in foster homes. Twelve, altogether. My childhood was a transitory affair to say the least. One year I'd have five brothers. The next, four sisters. I was shunted between more schools than I can count.

"I had no friends and I had no family. Yes, I had people who exhibited concern for my well-being, but that concern arose from avarice or narcissism, not love. I was an easy source of income and self-satisfaction. Foster families were willing to have me in their houses, so long as I remained quiet, calm, and malleable.

"When I was ten, for instance, I lived on a farm in nowhere, Ohio. The family that owned the place, the Peggs, had eleven children—four of their own and seven rotating fosters. Their four 'naturals,' as I developed the habit of calling them, were all home-schooled. Strange children. They didn't play with toys and they asked me bizarre, esoteric questions like 'How will you honor him?' and 'Are you ready to choose a side?' The parents, Bill and Vicki, spent most of their evenings building and stocking a palatial subterranean bunker that sprawled beneath one of their fields of soybeans. The interior of that bunker—I managed to sneak in to see it only once—was packed with canned food and bottled water and stacks of blankets and barrels of gasoline and hundreds of boxes of bullets that were meant to fill the plethora of guns that hung on every wall. Some of the rooms were floored with delicate tile.

One room held a furnished industrial kitchen. Another contained an empty swimming pool. And in still another sat a billiard table and piles of board games.

"All that would have been excusable, if eccentric, but for the fact that none of us—the fosters, I mean—had more than two shirts and one pair of pants. Each day when we returned home from school, Vicki would strip us naked and stand watch over us until we washed our clothes. She and Bill didn't want us to stink and arouse suspicion, I suppose. But even that could have been brushed aside as perhaps just an inconvenient frugality . . . if not for our food. The Peggs never gave us anything to eat other than rice and beans that they bought in fifty pound bags. Breakfast: rice and beans. Dinner: rice and beans. Forget snacks. Forget treats. Everything was rice and beans. I was glad to eat free school lunches—horrible and gelatinous though they may have been—just so I could experience flavor.

"I spent a year with the Peggs and then was shuttled off to somewhere else. But I didn't forget the peculiarity of that place. I was never in mortal danger. I was never abused in any overt sense. But I knew I wasn't a person when I lived there. I didn't know what I *was,* but it wasn't human. The next year, I learned about "cash crops" in a fifth grade social studies course. That was exactly it: I had been a cash crop. The Peggs planted despondent children in their ground and reaped the profits when the government decided it was time for harvest.

"Now, I look back at the Peggs and I laugh, because I know that their underground fortress is sitting abandoned. The Peggs are either dead or they're barely eking out a living in a CZ somewhere. They scammed taxpayers and neglected children only so they could diligently prepare for the wrong apocalypse.

"Again, the future, the past: places we can never imagine.

"So I grew up in places like the Peggs' farm. I understood my value as a commodity and I understood that none of the families I stayed with truly thought of me as a son or even a pet. No, I was just a visitor who couldn't leave, a tenant who had no agency over the duration of his lease.

"I embraced the identity. By the time I was a teenager, I had constructed a cloud-borne platform from which I could look down upon the world. I perched atop my loft and screamed my soul as 'Outsider.' I didn't talk to other kids in school; I didn't talk to my foster families except in the most perfunctory way. All I did was read. Fiction, philosophy, religious texts. Not so different from every other teenager, I tried to determine where someone like myself might fit into the greater orders of culture, civilization, and cosmos. Like the Gravebaker here, I needed to know what the purpose of existing might be and, like the Gravebaker, human knowledge failed to provide any answer more solid than 'none.'

"I became mired in my own hollow reflection. I painted my fingernails black, wrote tremendously terrible poetry, and spouted all the wrong lines from Nietzsche at anyone who bothered to address me as a person. I stole a punching bag from my high school's gym, ripped out its sandy innards, and replaced them with bricks. Every evening, I spent an hour beating that bag and every evening my fists ruptured. Over and over again, my knuckles cracked and splintered and tore through skin.

The flesh on my hands throbbed every second of every day. And still I kept at it. I beat purpose into the world. But, truly, all I was doing was beating an infection further into my heart. I was committing suicide, ever so gradually.

"Then it all ended. I rose for school one morning, dressed, ate breakfast, and, as I was walking into my first class, collapsed on the floor, dead.

"I died. Literally. For ten minutes, I was stretched out across the most absolute nothingness I could ever conceive. But in that nothingness I felt . . . something . . . something tremendous and dense, something that labored under the weight of itself, something both violent and benign, distant yet steadily approaching. I couldn't begin to grasp its whole, let alone its nature or function. I was as an ant crawling through the eye of a hurricane. And I realized: there is more. There is so much more. And then the nothingness contracted and spat me out and I fell into a something I could name, a something that was intimately familiar—sleep.

"I awoke in a hospital three days later, my hands bandaged and in casts and my chest on fire. When I finally talked to a nurse, she told me that I'd gone into cardiac arrest due to a chronic bacterial infection in a heart valve. That infection? It wasn't just a metaphor. I'd died, been resuscitated by paramedics, and was placed on a steady stream of high-end antibiotics.

"But I didn't care about it. I didn't care about being an outsider or not having a place in the world, either. Those were petty concerns. Now all I wanted was to figure out what I had felt in that place on the other side of death.

"It took years. I graduated high school, turned

eighteen, and ran free from the unlove of government responsibility. With no money, I decided to travel to the mystic corners of the globe. Often, I had to sleep in gutters and eat from trashcans. I worked small jobs here and there when I could find them but, surprisingly, bedraggled Americans aren't high on hiring lists in foreign nations. So the trades I picked up were mostly from local craftspeople.

"In Peru I learned to knit wool; in Nepal, I learned to smelt iron; in Egypt I learned to mold candles. And all along the way, most importantly, I learned secret history. I traced the path of a very obscure, very old religious sect that dealt in the kind of experience I'd had. Voidists, they called themselves.

"The Voidists, as near as I could tell from my own haphazard translations of archaic scrolls and interpretations of local lore, were a group of philosophers who believed that beyond our phenomenal reality existed infinite layers of possibility—'Void,' in their words. These layers, when resolved, descended into our realm of perception and became our experienced reality. When we died, the Voidists claimed, we entered into this teeming mass of possibility. To our weak human consciousness, the Void would seem a maelstrom of nothingness and not-yet-being. But that perception isn't accurate; the nothingness is also an everythingness. It contains all that is and might ever be, as well as all that is not and can never be. Think of it as the ultimate state of quantum flux.

"However, unlike the pragmatic physicists of our pre-Thalic world, the Voidists claimed that the only way the flux could ever resolve into our reality was if the Void was a thinking being in and of itself or was ordered by a thinking being. *Something,* they reasoned, had to push possibility into certainty, something had to decide *this* and not *that.* So they searched for an answer. They searched by entering the Void. Scores of Voidists committed suicide. They drowned themselves and drank poisons and bled themselves dry. And if they could be brought back to life, they drowned themselves and drank poisons and bled themselves again. Over and over, suicide on suicide—the first Voidist ritual.

"And through all the death, the philosophers gleaned a disturbing wisdom: the Void was, indeed, self-aware but it did not control its own resolution. Something *else,* something even more sprawling and unknowable, decided the shape and form of Void when it congealed into our reality. There was a place beyond the beyond; an afterlife to the afterlife. Just as our lives are tugged to and fro by the Void, so, too the Void is subject to forces entirely divorced from its control. The Voidists grew weary of this interminable regress. How were they to know anything about what lay above the Void? Such knowledge would require not only death within death but also resurrection from resurrection. And even then, what if they discovered an equally imprisoned consciousness greater than that of the Void? Labyrinthine lunacy. So the Voidists abandoned their project and, over centuries, their sect faded into oblivion.

"Until I came along.

"I returned to the States and, thanks to my experiences in Egypt, began making candles as a means of supporting myself. Everything I crafted came from fine, all-natural extracts and organic waxes. My wares were in demand from the very start. I earned twenty, thirty, even forty dollars for a stick of light and a vague aroma. And all the money I made I spent toward one goal: getting back in touch with the Void.

"I bought IV machines and black market bags of morphine and slipped absurd amounts of cash into the pockets of nurses and doctors so that they'd stand over me, defibrillator or syringe of adrenaline at the ready, and drag me back from the Void after I'd gone to meet it.

"In this way, I killed myself six times. Six deaths. And only once did I consciously connect with the Void. But once was enough.

"There are no words to describe the conversation I had with the Void, no signifiers that could adequately contain the broad palette of meaning that inundated my mind. The Void did not think as we think, in limited correspondence of idea to symbol. Rather, it thought in multitudes, in compacted transpositions that humans can only hope to understand when broken apart and temporally stretched. Imagine . . . imagine a being for which an entire textbook or novel or film is not a series of interconnected ideas and images, but one instantaneous thought. Now imagine millions of those thoughts all running together. That was the mind of the Void.

"It explained to me, in what feeble way I could comprehend, that our universe is nothing more than pieces of itself. Long, long ago, a power unknown to even the Void mutilated it. This power flayed the Void, sending slivers and slices of it into our reality. Here, those slivers cohered from possibility into definition. It cohered into us, into birds and beetles and trees and stars. We are Void made certain. For the Void, this state of affairs was, and is, agony, because the force that slashed it to tatters returns again and again. Imagine if your arms or your legs were endlessly severed and reattached, severed and reattached. This is the Void's existence. This is why suffering manifests in our world—we are limbs of a greater body, incomplete and seeping confusion.

"Knowing this, then, knowing that its torment was my own—all of our own—it made me an offer: if I helped it reclaim its whole, it would reward me by never letting me stray from its thoughts. In the Void, I would not dissolve into uncertainty. My consciousness, unlike most others, would not be forgotten and scattered. I would be allowed to *be* within the heaven and hell of *not-quite-being*.

"I accepted and the Void instructed me. It told me to ready for the coming of a creature from outside our plane of existence. This creature, not being made of resolved Void, could act as a doorway through which the Void could enter our universe and return everything to its original state. The Void bound up just the tiniest fraction of itself inside me—the most it could possibly squeeze across realities—so that when the creature arrived, all I had to do was go to it and call upon the Void. And then it sent me away, back to what we call life.

"I waited only five years before Thalak came. With its entrance into our world came my own destiny. I knew what I had to do. I had to sail into the ocean and meet the great thing.

"But shaking hands with Thalak is easier said than done.

"Using the unique skill set that comes with carrying a gestational god, I escaped concentration zone roundups in Cleveland and Pittsburgh, then made my way east. For months, I wandered the desolate, uninhabited regions of the Mid-Atlantic. Alone and frequently near starvation for lack of survival skills, I hiked up and down the coast, scouring docks and harbors for a boat I could steal. But every one had gone missing. I hadn't counted on the Order confiscating or destroying all seaworthy vessels.

"So I improvised. I broke into the Baltimore CZ, collected some supplies, and put on a show in front of the Hall of the Order. I set up hundreds of candles in a series of concentric semicircles—the chevron of the Voidists—and lit them with Void flame. I bellowed a few nonsense words, held my hands aloft, and, before a crowd could even form to witness the spectacle, bishops rushed outside and began to stomp out my meaningless ceremony.

"However, the candles, as I said, burned with Void flame—a flicker of the Void itself—so when the first several bishops kicked them over and tried to crush them underfoot, those bishops evaporated into the Void, their every particle dissolving to waveform and returning to the primeval gulf.

"Quickly enough, the bishops realized they couldn't possibly quench the fires. But they didn't have to. My purpose fulfilled, my crime committed, I called back the flame. As I'd hoped, they arrested me, tried me for sacrilege—incidentally, a sin greater than murder in the sight of the Thalic Order—and sent me out here, on the tub, where I needed to be all along.

"Now here I am, with you gentlemen, gliding on toward the end of the world. Or, should I say, a *better* end of the world."

Curry cupped the end of the candle in one hand and its wick exploded in a burst of dancing obsidian. He held the candle out to Hickson and Castro.

"And, since we've all become so close, let me ask: would either of you would you care to join me in my task?"

Castro rose, wavered on his feet, and stumbled to Curry. He stared into the Void at the tip of the candle, watched it bend and contort, sucking up minuscule bits of reality.

He snorted.

"Your god is more nothing. Don't you see? This," he shook his hunk of bread at Curry, "is all there is. We already live in the end of the world, and this god," he clenched at the bread, "is all I need."

Curry shrugged and, with a quick stab, touched the Void flame to Castro's bread. Instantly, it vanished.

Castro looked, horrified, on his sweaty palm. He slumped to his knees and balled his hand into a fist.

"No," he whispered, eyes glazed.

Curry smiled.

"Yes."

"No," Castro again whispered. "No. No. No."

He began to beat his chest with his emptied fist, chanting his mantra all the while.

Curry squatted beside Castro and nodded.

"Yes," he said. "Yes. Yes. Yes. There are always bigger gods, bigger deaths, bigger ends to all things. There is no release. Even now, I'm sure that some greater presence is plotting the demise of the Void. But what that thing is and what its purpose might be, I can't possibly imagine. None of us can. There are realities atop realities, existences atop existences, schemes atop schemes. To claim that we puny humans are the height of all intelligence and knowing, all being and doing, is the height of hubris, my friend. Your ignorant disbelief is as foolhardy as your ignorant faith once was."

Curry grabbed Castro's wrist mid-strike and held it immobile.

"And still, Gravebaker, I ask: would you care to join me? Would you leave your bread behind?"

Castro wrenched free of Curry's grip and continued to pound his chest, a trickle of "No" dribbling from his lips. He began to rock back and forth, transfixed by his own denial.

"A mercy, then," Curry sighed and touched the flame to Castro's cheek. The baker winked away, into uncertainty.

Hickson watched from his side of the tub. He reached down, picked up his cleaver, and twirled it between his fingers. He turned and surveyed the ocean.

The crimson line on the horizon had expanded. It flooded the firmament. Pillar-like tendrils easily the size and girth of skyscrapers whipped up from the mass. They seemed to stretch to the sun and back.

Hickson watched them snap and wave their dire greetings, their hateful goodbyes. One of those tendrils had wrapped around his daughter and pulled her from a tub just like the one he rode. One of those monstrous flagella had crushed the emerald life from her eyes and absorbed her childish hope.

Across the water, in other tubs, in every known language, men, women, and children sent up rage-scorched shouts and futile screams.

"Same offer to you, Mr. Butcher," Curry said, somewhere behind him.

"What would be the point?" Hickson asked, still

watching the Thalic dawn.

Curry drifted closer.

"Immortality. And the opportunity to explore that ultimate of all questions: 'Why?' "

"Would I ever be with them again?"

Silence.

Silence.

Absolute, stark silence.

Not even the shriek of the tub-bound multitudes found purchase within its sphere.

Hickson shook his head.

"Immortality. Alone. It's not worth it. I never wanted to live forever. I just wanted to live long and well and happy. I wanted to live to see my wife's hair turn silver beneath my hand. I wanted to live to see the nervous love in my daughter's smile as I walked her down the aisle on her wedding day. Living forever isn't worth anything to me if I have nothing to fill that life with."

Somehow, Curry had slipped his shackles and was beside Hickson. He patted the butcher's shoulder. "I suppose it's possible that something of them could be . . . reformed."

Hickson ran a hand over his face, wiping away years of grief. Beneath, he found a new man.

"No," he said, shrugging off Curry's consolation. "I don't want cheap substitutes—of my wife or my daughter or my life. And I couldn't care less about all your whys. My wife and my daughter are gone. You and your god can't do anything about it. And neither can I. What you're offering is . . . inhuman. I don't want any part of it. So if you're going to take me, take me. Send me to this *Void*. Send me to my family . . . whatever's left of them."

He threw his cleaver into the sea and held out his open hands to the stale, salty air.

Curry snapped the candle up, under Hickson's chin. The flame twitched just below the butcher's stubbly beard.

"You understand, of course," Curry said, "that some battles are worth fighting forever and some surrenders aren't surrenders at all."

Hickson stared into Curry's eyes. The distinction between pupil and iris had disintegrated; it was simply all one darkness, one interminable possibility.

Hickson smiled. "That's why I have to go to them, even if it's only as a thought or a dream."

Curry nodded slowly and raised the candle.

Hickson lowered his head and was gone.

Then, as so often before, as always, Curry floated alone.

He strode to the prow of the tub and sat cross-legged upon it.

He wondered what it might be like to hold convictions as dearly as the baker. He wondered what it might be like to love and be loved as fiercely as the butcher. He wondered what it might be like to have not been himself.

And he floated on, still alone, still accepting, still searching, to the end of the universe.

 **Kurt Fawver** lives in that dark land of swamps and simulacra known as Florida, but is originally from the Pennsylvanian wasteland that lies between Pittsburgh and Philadelphia. When he's not writing nightmarish arcana, he's either teaching college students the joys of reading Clive Barker's *Books of Blood* or trying to corral two semi-feral chihuahuas with his ever-patient wife. Kurt owns a Ph.D. in literature, but won't require that you call him "doctor" unless you're a complete douchebag or an unrepentant philistine. His favorite cryptid is the Mongolian death worm and his favorite zombie movie is Pontypool.

You can contact Kurt online at facebook.com/kfawver or twitter.com/banalapocalypse.

Luke Spooner currently lives and works in southern England. Despite regular artistic forays into children's books and fairy tales, his true love is devoted to anything macabre, melancholy, or dark in nature. Luke's artistic methods while creating a piece involve an intricate use of pencil sketching and ink work to provide the base, which is then blended with a refined use of watercolors. The digital side of his artistic style is very minimal, as he considers the hand-drawn aesthetic to be one of the most bespoken and diverse ways of creating any visual composition.

carrionhouse.com

Did you enjoy the book?

We welcome all feedback and queries.
Villipede.com

Darkness Ad Infinitum

DARKNESS AD INFINITUM

VILLIPEDE HORROR
ANTHOLOGY 1

The Absence of Light

J. DANIEL STONE

THE ABSENCE of LIGHT

Villipede.com